BEST EVER
101
Lawyer
Jokes

Matthew Burgess
Illustrations: Dyan Burgess

National Library of Australia Cataloguing-in-Publication entry

Creator:	Burgess, Matthew, author.
Title:	101 Lawyer Jokes / Matthew Burgess ; illustrator, Dyan Burgess.
ISBN:	978-1-925181-98-2 (createspace)
	978-1-925181-99-9 (Kindle)
	978-1-925181-31-9 (Smashwords)
Subjects:	Lawyers--Humor.
	Law--Humor.
	Practice of law--Humor.
Other Creators/Contributors:	Burgess, Dyan illustrator.
Dewey Number:	808.87

Published by D & M Fancy Pastry Pty Ltd
101 Lawyer Jokes
Copyright 2015 Matthew Burgess

Important disclaimer

Without limiting the rights under copyright reserved above, no part of this publication may be reproduced, stored, or transmitted in any form or by any means, without prior written permission of both the copyright owner and the above publisher of this book.

The information in this book is of a general nature and is intended to be (at least for some) humorous. It is not intended to be professional advice.

The book is a collection of jokes provided to the author over time and no offence is intended in relation to any aspect of the book.

The author also wishes to convey that this is a book of jokes. It should not be taken out of context and items mentioned should not be tried or actually done. This book is merely for entertainment purposes.

Contents

Chapter 1: Court Room	5
Chapter 2: The Billable Hour	22
Chapter 3: One Liners	33
Chapter 4: Q & A	37
Chapter 5: Story time	46
Chapter 6: Partners	68
Chapter 7: Heaven	106
Chapter 8: Adults Section	118
About the Author	137
Acknowledgement	139

Best Ever - 101 Lawyer Jokes

An Oldftyle Tales Prefs Original Publication.

The
YELLOW BOOKE

VOLUME I.
OCTOBER MMXIV.

*Contemporary Weird Fiction, Ghost Stories, Fantasy,
& Other Tales of Horror, Hauntings, Mystery, & Murder*

Edited by
M. Grant Kellermeyer

COLLECTED CONTENTS

The Afterwalk	C.M. Muller
Two Islands	M. Grant Kellermeyer
The Tragic Death of a Small Hunger	Robert Subiaga Jr.
Talking About the Old Days	Thomas Olivieri
Walking Directions Are in Beta: Use Caution	M. Grant Kellermeyer
Old Shock	David Senior
The End Has No End	Geoff Woodbridge
The Barrier: Nits in the Eyebrow	Don Swaim
Lost and Found	M. Grant Kellermeyer
A Closed Door	Geoff Woodbridge
The White Flower	Jeff Baker
Bedtime Story	Thomas Oliveiri

INTRODUCTION
— M. Grant Kellermeyer

THE following tales demonstrate a deep and passionate allegiance to the tradition of the classic tale of horror. Some are written by authors who have never been in print, some by professional authors, and some by published writers who have not tried their hand at horror before, but all are fans of the Gothic literature which has mystified and titillated generations of readers. Men wearing periwigs and tricorne hats and women in petticoats and stomachers hid dog-eared editions of the sensational Horace Walpole, sentimental Mrs Radcliffe, and decadent "Monk" Lewis in discreet places, saving them for the dark hours when their household had turned into bed and they could light a candle and read without fear of interruption or embarrassment. In a different century, the sooty streets of London were filled with middle-classed merchants and housewives rushing over gritty cobblestones with the ghost stories of Wilkie Collins, J. S. Le Fanu, Amelia B. Edwards, Rhoda Broughton, Charles Dickens, and Mrs Oliphant clutched shamelessly in their hands, looking forward to opening up the magazine during their journey home by hansom, carriage, or train car. Within another seventy years the philosophical sensationalism of Lovecraft, Hodgson, Machen, Chambers, Ashton Smith, Derleth, and Bloch were lovingly collected by adolescent boys, bored playboys, and jaded war veterans whether Wall Street was booming and gangsters running rough-shod over the law, or whether the soup lines stretched gloomily down city streets and Europe was darkening under the shadow of a new war. The novels of Bram Stoker, Mary Shelley, Robert Louis Stevenson, and H. G. Wells, the collections of Oliver Onions, M. R. James, E. F. Benson, and Ambrose Bierce, and the strange legacies of Hoffmann, Edgar Allan Poe, Henry James, Nathaniel Hawthorne, and Washington Irving haunted the personal libraries, nightmares, and imaginations of many thousands and even millions of artistically-endowed spirits: painters, illustrators, sculptors, playwrights, story tellers, novelists, musicians, composers, philosophers, critics, poets, historians, and the overlooked participant of art – the passionate reader. This collection has been designed and engineered by those same spirits. Some offer chilling homages to their literary heroes – Ambrose Bierce, M. R. James, William Hope Hodgson, E. F. Benson, J. S. Le Fanu, and others – which both emulate their styles and develop creatively upon their legacies. Some offer thoroughly unique and original works that challenge the conventions of the horror tale, building past the expectations and boundaries of classic speculative fiction. Some of the tales – you should be warned – are humorous. Some are farcical. Some are merely eerie, dark meditations. Some are wholesale landscapes of gruesome horror. Some are found documents. Some are disjointed narratives. One is a bedtime story. But all are sacrifices upon the altar of the tradition of the classic horror story, and all are pleasantly terrifying, and deliciously weird.

M. GRANT KELLERMEYER
FORT WAYNE, INDIANA, FALL 2014

AUTHOR BIOGRAPHIES

DON SWAIM

I am the founder and editor of The Ambrose Bierce Site, (http://donswaim.com) dedicated to the myth and mind of that caustic icon of imaginative fiction. While Bierce was an early influence, so were Ray Bradbury (I still have my first paperback edition of Fahrenheit 451) and Stephen Vincent Benét whose weird fiction, such as "By the Waters of Babylon" and his chilling nightmare poems were fodder for a teen like me. My own fiction and articles have appeared in small publications, on the Internet, and as ebooks, and my novel about H.L. Mencken (originally published by St. Martin's Press) was recently republished as an Authors Guild's backinprint trade paperback. Hundreds of my long-running daily CBS Radio features on books and authors, "Book Beat," can be heard on the Internet at http://donswaim.com/bookbeatpodcast.html. A career broadcast journalist, I'm also the founder of the venerable Bucks County Writers Workshop in Pennsylvania.

GEOFF WOODBRIDGE

The Yellow Booke will be Geoff Woodbridge's first outing into published writing. He has been writing short fiction for some time, alongside an English Literature degree. Inspired by a wide range of classics, The Bronte Sisters, Machen, Bradbury, and Voltaire, his work also echoes an influence, that of film, theatre and music. His working background is media critique and performance management. He is currently working on a novel alongside a collection of his dark fiction. Geoff resides in Liverpool with his Fiancé and his Rare Black Setter.

JEFF BAKER

Jeff Baker has worked in fast-food where he once had to dress up as a lobster; performed comedy in local clubs and driven delivery trucks carrying everything from amaretto to zucchini. He has been published in the anthologies "Zombie Lockdown" and "These Vampires Don't Sparkle." A 1983 graduate of Newman University, he lives in Wichita, Kansas with his Significant Other Darryl and "way too many" Hawaiian shirts. His Facebook page is at "Jeff Baker, Author."

Some of his favorite authors are Ramsey Campbell, August Derleth, Henry Kuttner, Wm Hope Hodgson (a direct influence on "The White Flower") and H.P. Lovecraft.

THOMAS OLIVIERI

Thomas is an accomplished ne'er-do-well and wastrel of renown -- he lives, writes, and loves in a state of serene frenzy. Edgar Allan Poe, Nathaniel Hawthorne, and M. R. James are some of his favorite authors and influences.

DAVID SENIOR

David Senior is a writer and photographer who lives in Norfolk, England. Inspired by the writings of MR James, HP Lovecraft, WG Sebald and Dennis Cooper, he has written a short novel called "The Sinners of Crowsmere." He runs the website 'EastScapes: The Abandoned, the Curious, and the Forgotten in East Anglia' at eastscapes.blogspot.co.uk, a base for images and writings about East Anglian folklore, (psycho)geography, and forgotten histories.

He is a lifelong fan of horror cinema, experimental writing, old sad songs best played in the small hours, broken toys, medical curios, and damp faded photographs found in the middle of nowhere. He intends one day to learn how to play the banjo.

ROBERT SUBIAGA JR.

Robert Subiaga Jr. is an educator and occasional science/communications consultant working out of the Mojave Desert in far-southern Nevada. Originally a native of Minneapolis-Saint Paul, his forays into creative work include a fair amount of various poetry/spoken word performances, the 1993 novel Eyes (which he hopes to soon re-release as a self-published e-book), and being writer/executive producer of the 2005 short film The Gnostic, starring the late Francesco Quinn (based on the prologue of another of Subiaga's novels to come out soon as an e-book). That is, when he's not chucking it all for open-topped Jeep rides across the West, camping out in "haunted" places as a vainly ghosthunting skeptic, or coaching youngsters how to slip the finer points of catch wrestling into their high school matches.

C. M. MULLER

C.M. Muller lives in St. Paul, Minnesota with his wife and two sons—and, of course, all those quaint and curious volumes of forgotten lore. He is distantly related to the Norwegian writer Jonas Lie, and draws much inspiration from that scrivener of old. In addition to writing, he enjoys the fine art of bookmaking, and has produced numerous volumes in just that manner. His first published tale appeared in the 2014 edition of Shadows & Tall Trees. Another is slated to emerge via Supernatural Tales in 2015. Visit him online at: http://chthonicmatter.wordpress.com.

Favorite Horror Writers:
Present: Simon Strantzas, Jason A. Wyckoff, Clint Smith
Slightly Past: Dennis Etchison, T.E.D. Klein, Terry Lamsley
Further Past: Robert Aickman, Shirley Jackson, Thomas Owen

THE AFTERWALK
— C.M. Muller

NORMAN Abfalter was admitted to Sunrise with a broken hip one month to the day after his wife of fifty-two years had taken up permanent residence there. As fate would have it, Iris's roommate had passed the morning prior to his arrival, leaving the only available bed in the facility. The arrangement was not dissimilar to the one they had grown accustomed to at home: separate beds, a nightstand for their things. The only noticeable difference was the long gray curtain dividing them from one another.

It had been an exhausting year for Abfalter. Iris's slow decline had proved mildly humorous at first, as she took the beginning stages of memory loss with that good grace and humor which had initially attracted him during their early courtship. But there had come a point when her forgetfulness resulted in unpredictable bouts of mental and physical abuse that hollowed his reserve in less time than he would have imagined.

The couple had no children, so the burden fell to Abfalter alone. And while aid did filter in from friends and neighbors, the well-wishes never seemed quite enough. Most outsiders did not fully comprehend how devastating it was to witness the degeneration and eventual loss of a lover's bond so many years in the making. It was catastrophic on all fronts, and Abfalter prayed many a night for his own mind to go.

Which is why the decision to admit Iris to Sunrise came as such a welcome reprieve. This did not mean that he ceased all contact (for he visited on a near daily basis), but being able to remove himself from the facility any time he wished and return to the house he had built half a century ago made life slightly more tolerable—until this, too, began to feel heartbreakingly empty.

Part of Abfalter still wondered if his misstep on the first rung of the grand stairwell (which had precipitated a death-defying tumble to the main level) had been premeditated by a hidden desire to either end his days or spend the remainder of them with the woman he loved.

The woman who no longer recalled his name.

* * *

Entering Sunrise that afternoon by wheelchair, Abfalter could not resist joking with the orderly about the bonds of marriage. The attendant laughed and Abfalter would have too, save for the discomfort he knew such an act would cause. Wheeling into his new room, the first thing he glimpsed was his wife being spoon-fed by a nurse. While Iris appeared to be looking directly at him, she made no acknowledgement of his presence. If anything, the man in the portable chair was merely another ghost come to haunt her. After this, Abfalter was not in such a joking mood. In fact, he was already wishing he had selected a different facility in which to convalesce.

As the orderly carefully transferred him from chair to bed, Abfalter was thankful for the long gray curtain separating the room. It made the task of imagining himself alone all the easier. Dr. Wilkoff had informed him that the hip would require up to a full year to heal, but that his stay at Sunrise needn't extend beyond a month. As he lay there thinking about this, Abfalter wondered if his sanity would hold. A month seemed an inordinate stretch of time, particularly when his mobility was so limited and his environs so disagreeable.

He summoned a nurse and politely requested a sedative.

* * *

Upon waking the following morning, Abfalter became briefly confused as to his whereabouts, having momentarily forgotten the details of his incarceration. The sedative he had taken the previous evening had been powerful enough to send him early to bed, and being out for so long had played havoc on his memories—regrettably not permanently.

The sun rising over the distant tree line created a portrait in the bay window that lifted Abfalter's spirits to a small degree. Yesterday, he had been able to joke about his admittance, but today the reality (and length) of his imprisonment chilled him to the core. The quiet house he had left behind now struck him as a veritable paradise.

He reached for the remote on the nightstand, figuring that a news program would take his mind off things. In doing so his attention was drawn to the opposite half of the room. At some point during the night, the curtain had been drawn just enough to display the upper portion of Iris's bed. She was looking directly at him.

"Morning, sunshine," Abfalter said, after the initial shock. "Sleep okay?"

Iris continued to stare, the intensity of her gaze almost too unnerving to hold. Her eyes seemed darker than Abfalter remembered, although he was quick to reason that this was due to the rather minimal lighting on her side of the room. Still, he began longing for a nurse to arrive, simply to have the curtain returned to its original position.

"You look familiar," Iris whispered. "So very…familiar."

The awkwardness of the situation proved too much for Abfalter. He returned his attention to the television, attempting no further discourse with the stranger across the divide.

Thankfully, a nurse arrived not long after with his breakfast. As she turned to go, Abfalter asked that the curtain be drawn.

* * *

Contrary to his opinion of institutional cuisine, Abfalter rather enjoyed the meal. His own attempts at cooking, once Iris had gone away, proved both frustrating and non-nutritious. Now, with a bit of dietary regulation back in his life, the likelihood of recovering inside of a month seemed more than a distinct possibility.

Dr. Wilkoff, when he arrived for his morning visit, offered no encouragement in this regard, reiterating that the convalescence would last at least a month, and probably more. He then asked, "How are you getting on with the room situation?"

Abfalter put on a facade of fortitude, stating that everything was first-rate.

The good doctor read beyond the ebullient reply, suggesting that a transfer to another room was entirely possible, particularly if the living arrangement made him uncomfortable. Abfalter scoffed at the idea, but thanked the physician nevertheless.

"We're all pulling for you, Norman," Dr. Wilkoff said before taking his leave.

Abfalter stared at the opposite wall, searching for but failing to resurrect memories of his early life with Iris. He shifted angrily, desperate to find the remote. Pain compressed his hip like a vise-clamp and he gritted his teeth against the profanity vying to break through.

"Nor-man?" The voice beyond the curtain startled him, but had a recuperative effect as well. Abfalter sat stock-still, awaiting further confirmation that the youthful-sounding voice was not mere delusion. "Sweetheart?"

"I'm here, Iris," he whispered, rambling on about his arrival at Sunrise and how he had ended up in the same room. Talking at length felt invigorating, even if Iris was hidden from view. He used the opportunity to profess how much he missed her, how much he loved her.

He waited anxiously for a response, but none was forthcoming. Had he been capable of doing so, he would have proceeded to Iris's bedside; instead, he relied on the only option available: the call-button on the remote. He depressed it, cringing as the pain in his hip began to resurge.

A nurse, having seemingly materialized out of thin air, stood at his side.

"How was your breakfast, Mr. Abfalter?" she said. "I trust you slept well?"

Abfalter ignored the questions and pointed at the curtain. "If it's not too much to ask," he said, "I'd like to have a word with my wife."

The nurse gave an endearing smile, but in the end stated that Iris was resting soundly and should not be disturbed. As if to prove her point, she carefully parted a portion of the curtain to reveal a reposed and rather serene-looking Iris.

"I know how difficult this must be for you, Mr. Abfalter," the nurse said, returning to his side. "My own mother is going through much the same ordeal. When she—"

But Abfalter heard nothing more of what she had to say. He turned his attention to the bay window, attempting (not very successfully) to halt the onslaught of memory.

* * *

Spending so much time in a near horizontal position tested Abfalter's resolve to an astonishing degree. Never in his long life had he desired anything more than to simply rise up and move from point A to point B, even if that trajectory involved no greater distance than the threshold of his room to the reception desk.

Abfalter had never considered himself much of a reader, save for the occasional car repair manual when necessity struck, but as he rummaged through the top drawer of his nightstand, he uncovered a King James Bible. Second only to his disinterest in reading was organized religion, but the fact that the book was able to push his thoughts in another direction was enough to make him reconsider his stance (at least temporarily) on both topics. He had even devised a plan of sorts, which involved the number of pages he would need to daily consume in order to finish the lengthy tome before his release.

This, then, became Abfalter's sole and abiding focus. Barring mealtimes and numerous visits from the orderlies, he found more than enough time to fill his quota. Once done, he would smack the book shut and experience an almost electric thrill. He wasn't sure if this was due to the words themselves or the fact that he had accomplished the task, though perhaps it was a bit of both. What truly mattered was that the passing of days had begun to accelerate. A month no longer seemed so dreadful.

Nighttime was usually relegated to watching television, and one fortuitous evening he chanced upon a film which sparked an unexpected and powerful memory. The movie, starring Spencer Tracy and Katharine Hepburn, had been the first he and his soon-to-be wife had seen together. He had proposed to her shortly thereafter.

At no point during the picture did Iris stir, though at numerous points Abfalter extended a hand toward the curtain as if expecting the gesture to be returned.

* * *

He must have dozed at some point, for upon waking he recognized none of the images on the screen. It took him a moment, as well, to realize that the actors' voices were overlaid by another, more familiar one. He depressed the volume on the remote until the voice (which had a strangely submerged quality to it) could be heard.

"...mustn't worry dear mustn't fear I will cross over soon..."

Abfalter cursed his immobility, longing more than anything to be at his wife's side, to comfort her as he had so often in the past. The simple act of holding her hand would mean so much to him; and to her, he should imagine.

He encouraged Iris to continue, no matter how distressing her message. Receiving no response, he began to wonder if the voice had been nothing more than a telltale sign of his own looming dementia. He whispered, "I love you, Iris. More than you'll ever know."

A heartbeat later, he detected movement within the room.

First, a creaking from her bed; and second, a shuffling of slippers across the linoleum floor. Abfalter imagined Iris (for who else could it be?) charting a course through the darkness.

But when he squinted into the void, he noticed something else peering back.

While he could not make out its features, he sensed that it was staring directly at him. The shuffling commenced and as the form began to take shape in the nimbus of light cast by the television, Abfalter shielded his eyes and screamed.

The next thing he knew he was staring up at a nurse. She had him by the shoulders and was speaking in a soothing voice. Abfalter wasted little time inquiring about his beloved companion. The nurse smiled, stating that Iris seemed to have slept through the entire episode. She then handed over a sedative and wished him pleasant dreams.

Needless to say, Abfalter had no strong desire for sleep that night.

* * *

His first task the following morning was to request a room transfer, and by mid-afternoon that appeal was met. As much as it pained Abfalter to admit, he should never have allowed himself to be placed in the same room as Iris. Memories and his own feelings of isolation had turned the situation into a nightmare scenario, as evidenced by the strange dream he had experienced the previous evening. (During the long and sleepless night, Abfalter had convinced himself that it had been this and nothing more.)

When he was wheeled into his new room (which was on the same floor as Iris, but at the opposite end of the corridor), he was surprised to discover that he would have the space all to himself—at least until the end of the week, when a new resident was scheduled to join him. Abfalter joked with the orderly, stating that by the time this new roommate arrived he himself would be long gone. The attendant patted Abfalter on the back, bringing up the old saw about the Lord working in mysterious ways. He had no doubt noticed the book Abfalter had been holding like a talisman during the transfer.

The new room was a replica of the one he had just left, save for a slightly different view from the bay window. As Abfalter lay in bed, studying the details of a world he longed to rejoin, he could not help but think of Iris and his rather rash decision to abandon her over some ridiculous dream. He began flipping through the King James, but in the end threw it against the far wall—forgetting of course about his hip, which rewarded him with a torrent of pain.

Dinner was served not long after, and the nurse, noticing the book laying in her path, plucked it up and set it wordlessly at Abfalter's side. Her kindness (and the fact that she had delivered a particularly scrumptious meal) lifted his spirits considerably. He spent most of the evening (contrary to his earlier denunciation) reading his quota for the day, pausing now and again to admire the view beyond the pane.

Night arrived more quickly than he would have liked, and with it the sense of impending bad dreams. Staring at the darkened window, Abfalter wanted nothing more than to return in time to that place of eternal-seeming happiness which had once existed between himself and Iris. To take his mind off matters, he turned his attention to the television, which was only moments away from showcasing another familiar and memory-laden film. Mere mention of it nearly had him summoning a nurse to demand that Iris be wheeled to his side, close enough to clasp her hand. He missed her warm companionship. That he had abandoned her was unconscionable.

Near the end of the movie, Abfalter was already drifting in and out of sleep.

* * *

He opened his eyes and immediately sensed a presence at his side.

A barely discernible voice whispered something in his ear, attempting to communicate through a mouth to which it was still growing accustomed.

Abfalter remained strangely calm through it all. He reached into the darkness. "I've missed you so much. So very much…."

As contact was made, it felt as though numerous threadlike strands were cocooning his hand and wrist and rising by slow degree along his arm, his shoulder, his chest.

Soon his entire body would be subsumed by what Iris had become.

He welcomed her growing embrace with all his heart and soul.

TWO ISLANDS
— M. Grant Kellermeyer

THREE miles south of Berne, Indiana a very conventional bridge fills the gap caused by the yellow arm of the Wabash River that curls between Adams County and Jay County. This bridge has been worn white from the friction of school bus wheels and the heat of the sun which, at noon, is perfectly poised between the two hedges of shaggy woodland that sprout up on either side. Below, in the honey-colored mud (which, in winter and spring, is transformed into honey-colored sludge) two islands – one on either side of the bridge – sprout from the river bed like the backs of two men floating face-first in the brown water. Both are lean, made from mud which is reshaped every season by the erosion and waxing of the river tides – brittle and towering in the August heat, sleek and shapeless in the March rains. Grey shrubs and hair-like grass dangle from its banks, and a half a dozen limp saplings huddle in the center of each shifting blob. Canoes – which rarely venture into the dank shallows of the river's Adams County stretch – must carefully gauge the water when they pass the earthy masses, or risk becoming entangled in the greedy webwork of roots, tires, and branches that hover between the river bed and the opaque surface.

The westerly mound tended to be squat and thick, approximately the size of a tennis court, while the easterly protrusion – which followed the bend of the river and was crescent-shaped like a clipped thumbnail – was broad at the middle, tapering into horns, and was long enough to park fifteen large sedans end-to-end along its spiny meridian.

The bridge between them lay between my hometown and the middle-school that I attended. I was an intoxicated daydreamer during those years, and when the bus carried me between those shifting mud banks. To my young mind they were romantic: for a boy raised in the cornfields of east-central Indiana the prospect of an island of any kind evoked fantasies of pirates, treasure, forts, hideouts, campsites, and robbers. I imagined using them as a base of operations for summertime escapades – a place to camp, fish, and construct crude fortifications, never mind under whose jurisdiction or ownership the property fell. Not far from it, the Snow Cemetery – a resting place for local Civil War dead – rested sleepily: a hump of shaggy grass speckled with low, square rectangles washed white and nameless by time. It was curiosity to discover more about the history of these sunken graves and their bucolic surroundings that influenced me to sift through maps of the county and the river. I remember looking at old surveys of the river and being shocked to watch their steady development: in 1840 the river was broad and unblemished at that particular bend; a map from 1863 shows the crescent just peeking from the surface; in 1898 (a decade after the Civil War cemetery was planted near its banks) it is nearly entirely emerged; in 1942 the tennis court begins to show itself; in 1971 the transformation is complete. I was stunned at their apparent willfulness, sentience even. Ultimately I fetishized their romance found myself begrudging my unwillingness to either walk the three miles to explore them or ask my parents to drop me off – an option immediately excluded by the need for this adventure to be an exercise in independence and self-reliance, for that was what the two islands had come to represent to me.

Nolan and I were fifteen when we borrowed his cousin's canoe to cross the large, serpentine lake that formed the nucleus of Berne's semi-affluent neighborhoods. He later decided to join the Marines, and in retrospect it was natural that he found some affinity with the only substantial tract of grey water in the general vicinity. It was a manmade lake with beveled shores and symmetric outlines, dotted by two islands of its own – one football shaped, one baseball shaped – in separate wings of flat, safe water. The canoe Nolan borrowed – it ultimately became synonymous with our friendship as I in turn would then borrow it from him to scout Fryback Lake on weekday mornings in June and July – had a red, fiberglass hull edged in black plastic, with black plastic seats forward and astern. Propelled by two aluminum-shafted paddles with black fins and grips, it was a simple and stable craft, unthreatened by the subtle swells resurrected by distant speedboats and the gusts of wind that ruffled its surface during summer storms.

Where I was a romantic, Nolan was a genuine explorer, unburdened by imagination or expectation. His was merely to do and die, not to reason why, and his extroverted gumption quickly outpaced my thoughtful reflections in bringing my long-desired landfall to fruition.

We were eighteen and our final semester of high school had been underway for several months – it was early April – when we decided to promote the canoe, (which we self-importantly called *Intrepid* after my Dodge sedan) from lake maneuvers to river duties. The decision wasn't entirely unrelated to our quickening separation: Nolan was due to enter basic training in the summer of 2006, and I had been accepted to Anderson University. While neither of us mentioned the obvious, it was clear that – excluding chance encounters when college breaks and furlough coincided – our friendship was to be heavily abbreviated in the coming months.

We were at a campfire in his backyard – the perennial social space for any rural town during months with tolerable weather – with two or three of our common friends. *Intrepid* was perched behind us on a cord of snow-rotted firewood. A person who has little to do with this story – I'll call him Phil – was laying his hand on the pulpy mass and emptying his bladder into its midst. It is natural to suppose that Phil was in the process of converting lite beer from cold, pale fluid to warm, pale fluid, but this is not the case. A regular of our youth group, Phil was a determined teetotaler, and while he felt that it was his duty to act the ass (as a starring member of the varsity golf team), he did so entirely without the influence of liquor (what he imagined this would do for his reputation, I can't possibly suppose). Most often, this manifested itself in conspicuous semi-nudity in homosocial circles – streaking, public urination, non sequitur moonings, and the whole gamut of Christ-approved self-debasement). Once the cluster of girls – a group which perennially flitted in and out of our social circle without ever dating any of us – had disappeared into the same car and left for a rival bonfire on the rival side of town, Phil saw fit to, as he termed it, "take care of [his] bidniss," as he leaned into the woodpile. *Intrepid* hung over him like a divine grimace.

"Hey. What're you doing this Saturday?"

I looked up at Nolan. I was lost in thoughts of graduating, of losing my friends, and of finding a career.

"I don't know. I guess nothing, really. Why? What're you thinking?"

His eyes were simultaneously excited and hesitant, afraid of my response, I deduced. Phil had decided to shed his pants entirely and climb onto the pile. I ignored the spectacle which was apparently becoming a cause célèbre with the bonfire's three or four remaining attendants.

"I wanna take the canoe out on the river."

He wasn't paranoid to doubt a positive response; I was much likelier to risk cuts, bruises, wetness, hunger, and difficulty in my imagination, and I had turned down several dozen self-same suggestions (including being branded with a coat-hanger, detonating Works bombs, and playing football in the February snow) throughout our friendship. But the germ of an idea took root in my mind: I saw the weed-strangled mud banks whose independence had allured me since I can remember being driven over the bridge to school.

"Where at?"

"We can park the truck in Linn Grove and take it the Loblolly Creek Fork to Geneva."

The two islands squatted almost mathematically between the two points. My interest had been won. Nolan lacked his usual vigor, however. Something akin to nervousness flickered in his irises, and although it made me pause to wonder, I passed it by, contributing it to his approaching enlistment. I realized what the future posed for him, and I didn't envy the prospect of leaving the freedom of my clean avenues and quiet parks for the nocturnal firefights and broiling oil fields of Iraq. While he believed in his cause, and while he was suited to a life lived under the guidance of authority, the encroaching loss of his private citizenship had been weighing heavily on his spirit, and – or so I imagined – a foray onto the river, entirely free of commands or instructions, might ease his anxieties. Without asking I understood, and I decided that the sortie would be beneficial to both of our psyches, as he approached enlistment and I enrollment.

We would take *Intrepid* to Linn Grove (a virtual hamlet of some two dozen houses encircling one of the river's snake-like coils) in two days.

Phil's entourage had crowded around the woodpile, encouraging his display, when one of them – a phenomenally obese person – bent over in a jerking motion, losing their footing, falling against the wood. Turning roughly on his ankle to account for the shockwave, Phil reached for an invisible ladder before being displaced onto the ground some six feet below. I decided that this was an appropriate time to leave. Before turning my back to a naked and bruised Phil being helped from the ground by his noticeably less-enthused associates, I noticed that *Intrepid* had been dislodged during Phil's fall and decline: in the darkness I couldn't easily distinguish its black interior from the background of the woodpile, but I remember walking away with the impression that it resembled a lipless, toothless mouth, its jaws drawn back in desperate hunger.

In the meantime our lives followed their natural tracks: we met for coffee and pancakes with our friends on Friday mornings; we ran the gamut of classes – each somewhat entrapped and dwarfed in the gravity of graduation; we had petty responsibilities at home. And when Saturday morning came, we changed into grungy shorts and tees, slipping on canvas shoes, and bringing whatever trinkets we thought fitting with us in nylon rucksacks.

Once I had changed and rubbed the sleep from my hair and eyes, I burdened by ruck with a thermos of coffee, hatchet, a coil of nylon rope, and a meal of jerked beef, crackers, and apple slices preserved with lemon juice. It was nine o'clock and the sky was bluish-white, low and hefty. The promised rain wasn't due for another twenty hours, and I took the low ceiling in stride, announcing to myself that it was good, that I wouldn't have to worry for sunburn.

Nolan was already outside when I drove up. He had shouldered *Intrepid* into the bed of his truck and was climbing into the cab with his provisions slung over his back in a drawstring bag. I pulled up alongside his house, a brown ranch ensconced in well-trimmed turf, and called out to him. He shouted my name and jumped up and down excitedly. This wasn't the spirit with which I had hoped, as a ten year old boy, to gracefully make landfall on the court and crescent, but his enthusiasm was the fuel of our expedition, and I feigned the same degree of excitement, eager to leave the organized street plans of society for the Wabash's unfenced boulevard.

The truck ride to Linn Grove was long and anxious; I wondered how high the river was, whether we would be challenged by possessive property owners, if Nolan would respect my desire to land on the islands, or if his pragmatic character would insist that we shuttle up and down the river without pause for needless sentiments. Our friendship was based on our dovetailed senses of humor: where Nolan was a loud exhibitionist given to public stunts, I was a sharp-tongued whit, capable of augmenting his feats with the color of my imagination. Without him, I was a solemn mind. Without me, he was a braggish mouth.

We eased the pickup down a worn trail that lead down the bank of a subtle ditch, running parallel with the river for a quarter-mile. Once we were out of sight of the highway, entirely enveloped by the grey fingers of ash trees and beeches. The river was bloated with the previous month's snow and rain, making the prospect of canoeing simultaneously more practical and more deadly. The current was drawing black limbs past us at an uncommonly rapid pace, but both of our chests throbbed with the heat of exploration, and it is only in retrospect – after what I now know was to happen – that I recall the river's temperament. During the summer months the Wabash was a sickly, fetid ditch, but in the spring months it was quick and cantankerous. The caramel-colored water, frothing at the banks and boiling in long bands when impeded by refuse or downed limbs, was known to sweep over its boundaries in the middle of the night, dragging objects, flora, and fauna into its eager mouth when the floods subsided, quenching its angry hunger.

It was with great care that I lowered myself into *Intrepid* while Nolan steadied the stern. We had lowered it into a shallow sheltered from the current by a pile of grey tires, but it still rocked convulsively. I laid my rucksack in the center, taking up the forward paddle while Nolan slipped into the aft, releasing his hold on the shore, and – with an easy push from his paddle – injecting us into the foamy rush.

The current pulled us forward, and our paddles did little more than guide our path. I had never been this close to the Wabash, and the thrilling connection to the mythic waterway which embossed my state like a soldier's crossbelt, was existential. The water lapped hungrily at *Intrepid's* prow, thumping the bottom viciously as each swell passed under us. Fryback Lake had been domestic and ingratiating, like a man-slave purchased from the company of a conquered people, but the Wabash was barbaric and free, and it tossed us out of the way when we became too burdensome or demanding.

We rode the milky surface for several miles, talking over the humming voices that surrounded us, in high voices, exchanging petty jokes and cheap insults while we surged over the river's opaque atmosphere, crashing through spiny dams of ice-gutted branches and congealed bogs of black leaves and pine needles. We watched the white walls of Linn Grove pass us by, and the shape of the landscape changed subtly from distant brown fields to shaggy hills tangled with underbrush, crowned by the dun skeletons of ash trees.

It was three hours later when I recognized the irregular spacing of the trees and the glint of aluminum caught my attention. Through the nest of branches I could see the systematic, orderly architecture of the concrete bridge with its railing glinting in the cold white light of early April. It was there when I looked down and ahead: like a slumbering slug, profound in size and girth, the western horn of the crescent came into relief, black against the orange sludge.

"When do you wanna eat?"

"Huh?"

"Like lunch. We could land on one of these islands and eat."

"On our way back. Let's make it to Geneva before we stop."

I wasn't surprised, but I was annoyed. As *Intrepid* coasted alongside the crescent I was able to scan its shoreline – for the first time at eye level. It was wild and ragged, cluttered with fallen trees, and swollen with pulpy clay hillocks. A cluster of twigs clutched at the back of my neck as we glided under some of the stranger looking trees. I brushed them off. I remember having that same, fanciful sensation: the islands looked like two slumbering slugs, fat and well-fed. A low-hanging branch became caught on our prow, somehow without my noticing. I pushed it off with my paddle.

We rushed past the faceless hulks, passing through coil after coil of fermenting water, pausing only at the fork where the Loblolly Creek eased southerly towards Geneva. The difference was palpable. The embankments were grassier, lower, sleepier, and we cruised softly if not complacently across this quiet branch before beaching in a yellow bed of grass to stretch and snack. Nolan was nursing a Jones Soda when I reintroduced the topic of the two islands.

"Are you still thinking of lunching on that island?"

"Which one?"

I thought. The tennis court had seemed considerably compromised by the water —somehow slimy, even – barely more than a mud pie sprouting shags of grey grass.

"The longer one. Shaped like a moon."

"Okay, okay."

He seemed thoughtful, an uncommon state. His impulsivity had both benefitted and annoyed me, but the shift was so sudden that I was initially concerned before he responded.

"We'll make a fire there and have lunch."

"A fire?"

"I brought lighter fluid and newspaper."

I considered the potential laws we might violate, but laughed off my concerns. Wasn't this what I had imagined? Beaching a watercraft on that scraggly islet, making camp on its surface, claiming it for my own like a weary discoverer raising his country's colors over a wild and unclaimed territory? I agreed. We loaded back into *Intrepid*, paddling into the current, not noticing the purple streaks clotting the eastern sky.

The going was certainly rougher, even in the Loblolly, usually a passive tributary. We began to struggle once we rejoined the Wabash, dipping vigorously into the wash at sporadic intervals, avoiding the gnarled onslaught of driftwood and garbage. Overhead, after an hour in the water, we noticed the canopy of white, purple, and pale green leaflets shivering from some unseen disturbance. Shortly after, the upper portions of the trees began shifting drunkenly as a heavy wind rippled through them. Paying it no mind, we continued making hard-won progress, ladling the water aside with deep strokes. *Intrepid* bounced over the blackening swells, and after several hours of manhandling it between fallen ashes, over slushy leaf dams, and around the corroded bodies of bicycles, pushcarts, and tractor parts, we spotted the metalwork of the bridge, and saw the tennis court's sloughing membrane of purple mud. Passing it by, we paddled hard for the crescent.

After two vigorous strokes, we rammed *Intrepid* into the grey muck of a natural harbor on the crescent's northern bank, where the gap between island and shore was little more than the length of two men's bodies laid head to toe. I rapidly dismounted onto the ashy soil, dragging Nolan and *Intrepid* onto firm ground. Unloading our gear, we quickly settled down to eat, and – after five hours of labor – our meal was nearly more satisfying than the achievement of my childhood ambition.

In fact, now that I stood on the blackened clay, looking through the canopy of leafless, grey fingers, I was unsettled by its size and atmosphere. It was far larger than I had expected, a fact which would have delighted me to know, but standing in its domain, I found it disquieting and perverse. It stretched out on the river like a tumor of earth, gorging itself on nearby life. Indeed, none of the grotesque white bass and catfish, whose fungal bodies had regularly thudded against *Intrepid's* thin hull seemed to have followed us past the bend that exposed us to the two islands. Peering from its highest point I could see the blanched headstones of the Snow Cemetery and the long-faded American flags skewered into the earth. I noticed for the first time that a shallow ravine lead from the grave plot to the river, depositing a sluggish flow of brown water into the river surrounding the tennis court.

Nolan quietly rounded up a collection of weeds, twigs, and brush, forming it around a white chunk of wood that he had trimmed with my hatchet, stuffing paper between the gaps. He anointed it with lighter fluid, and set a flame to the bundle. After three attempts to sustain fire, a belt of blue smoke chugged from its center, and the wood began to ash and smolder. His energy was devoted to the fire and his mood was clearly one of somber introspection.

I crossed the island's spine, walking around the pools of tea-colored water and the shattered shells of tree boughs, taking in its simple but ponderous geography. I felt a thread-like root grab my ankle and shook it free, breaking it from the clay and walking on. No nests of birds, havens for geese, or even holes for water snakes were visible, only the coarse vegetation and a tractor tire embedded into the soil. Due to rain, erosion, and flooding, the tire was encased in purple mud which rejoined seamlessly with the island, making it appear to be as much a natural appendage of the crescent as a one of the subtle hillocks that bubbled along its meaty midriff. My shirt snagged on a splintered branch, and I unhooked it with my fingers.

Nolan sat with his hands on his knees, peering into the red light. It was then that I noticed how dark the sky had grown. Indeed, the air gave no hint of life-giving rain, but the winds were whipping across the backs of the trees, and a steady chorus of groans rose from their racked trunks which bobbed back and forth, and their boughs which clattered one against the other, or rubbed together, generating a cry like ice crushing steel plates.

"Will we have to stay out here until it clears up?" I asked.

He didn't look up.

"No, we'll leave the canoe here and hitch a ride from the highway if it comes down to that."

Hitch-hiking's distasteful connotations aside, I was surprised.

"It's not going to rain. I checked the weather channel just before I left. It's just windy. We probably should be on the river until the wind eases up."

He didn't look up.

"We'll get a ride if you don't want to paddle. We're not staying here much longer."

I was about to respond when I noticed the water levels rising sluggishly. Already the twelve foot gap between the crescent and the northern shore had expanded several feet. Storms in the south were glutting it with rain water, I supposed. Nolan was shaking his foot, untangling it from a band of white roots. I thought about my childhood fantasies. It *was* a romantic spot: a solitary giant, its belly and feet protruding through the caramel-colored water. While I stood on the belly, overlooking the receding shoreline, I felt a determination to spend at least one hour on the mound.

"I don't want to leave just yet."

"Why not?"

"It's nice to be just sitting here with the fire."

The bundle of weeds was still expectorating a series of white serpents, but its red light had shriveled protectively into its heart.

"What fire? Let's go. I don't like this place. It's—"

"Where's *Intrepid*?"

The canoe was not where it had been, upside down on the southern bank of the islet.

"God..."

"Where *is* it?"

"I don't know... Is it—?"

"There!" I shouted.

It was floundering in a tangle of great black beech roots nearly two hundred yards upstream; its red hull flashed urgently in the midst of the murk.

The sky overhead had become a series of bruise-hued clots which rushed frantically away from the driving wind.

"We have to get it."

"Get it? It will be fine; it's heading downstream, where we should be going now."

"How did it even get upstream? I mean against the current?"

"That's seriously the least of my—"

He swatted at a bundle of underbrush that clung to his waistband. I reached to unsnag it when I felt something thick and wet on my bare calf. My chest expanded with white heat and I tossed my body forward, flailing the offended limb until I noticed that the skin was bare. Bare, save for a triangular puncture that did not bleed.

I remembered something of what the island resembled when we first saw it, and I shuddered, my elbows clinging to my body.

"How are we going to get off?" I asked.

Parallel bands of leaden water rushed on either side – some twenty feet to the north, some forty to the south. Nolan was brushing something off of his knee.

"We swim."

{20}

I remembered the fungal catfish and felt my gorge rise. The river's pollutants were infamous; all of the farmers knew not to water their herds with Wabash water, and would have rather eaten spoiled meat than one of the river's dank large-mouth bass. The skies hurried past, grazing the tree branches with their sagging haze. I swatted at my neck, then my shoulder, feeling what I can only describe as spider's legs made of cold wood. I ignored the sensation, eager to distract myself.

"Swim. Okay. Okay. Let's get our shirts off."

As if in response to my directive, Nolan peeled the yellowed cotton from his back, exposing the fat, fungal slug that had affixed itself to his spine, between the shoulder blades. It was the size of well-fed cat, and I still cannot imagine how its weight didn't alert my friend. Unable to scream, I swung my head from side to side, hissing as hot tears stung my face. I couldn't bring myself to touch Nolan or to strike at the thing with a stick; I couldn't bring myself to acknowledge its corporeality – its basic existence.

Before I could think another perverse thought, I felt spiny wooden fingers trace the width of my own back. When, overcoming the paralysis of my shock, I turned to see the tree-ish thing, whose face I will never forget, I felt my lungs explode with hot air, and a scream tore from my sandy throat. Awoken to the threat, Nolan saw the leering thing – tree or skeleton, I still don't know what it was – and swung around in frenzied terror. I believe that this violent motion swung the slug-thing around, causing its weight to pull on the skin of his back, because his face shriveled with cosmic horror and his hands suddenly flew to his back, swatting hatefully at the blood-bloated thing. I rushed away from the tree-thing, and stooped to help my friend who had fallen to the ground in a fit, shaking and drooling. Beneath him the slug had been flattened, although its tail still twitched vindictively. Stunned and uncertain of my senses, I stood over his gyrating body and nearly fell into hysterics, but I saw the plump, grey membranes of some six or seven cat-sized polyps greasing their way across the clay, from the direction of the tennis court. In the water I could see several dark patches moving from the smaller islet's banks with serpentine dexterity, issuing forth like wakeful soldiers from a barracks.

I shook him into awareness and – without regard for the river's corrosive toxicity – we surged into the water and pulled ourselves towards shore, using the rope in my ruck to lash our torsos together. His weight was astounding under the circumstances, but I managed to keep his mouth above the water, and to drag him over the orange slush, past the things that reached out desperately for us. It was the spidery fingers which clutched at me from beneath the milky surface that almost ruined my mind – thin and probing, they plied at my skin – and the kittenish suckling at my ankle awoke me to the terror and propelled me forward.

We exited the water and stumbled stupidly onto the dull grass of a farmer's field. Before I dropped him and fell into the warm mud beneath me, I noticed three triangular wounds on my lower calves – white and bloodless.

Nolan was missing from class for a week, and I was unable to explain our experience until he had entered basic training and been sent to patrol the shores of the Euphrates in the summer of 2007, where the oil-fires blackened the desert sky. The doctors who examined us located a series of injuries, some like the bite of a leech, though unusually-shaped, large, and toxic, and others like the scratches of human nails – four in lateral lines and a fifth slightly to the side – though the lacerations were infested with wood fiber and splinters.

I haven't heard from Nolan since we graduated. He enlisted into military hungry for personnel, and I spent the next six years in school while the economy tumbled around me. I heard that he has led a successful, if short career in the Marines. He poured himself into action and impulse, eschewing imagination entirely, rising to the rank of corporal and earning the Purple Heart when his unit was hit my small arms fire on a night patrol. Whatever happened that night on the Euphrates, his mind had been more severely wounded than his body: he was insensible and had to be carried away from the black shores in a gibbering fit. After this action, he was psychologically evaluated and honorably discharged.

Intrepid was reclaimed from the river in Linn Grove, a quarter-mile south of where we launched it that morning. With the exception of a series of parallel scratches to the hull and a veneer of blackish slime, it was undamaged, although I know this only from Nolan's cousin: I have not asked to use the canoe since that April.

It was last year that I sat down with a friend from college (a quiet man who had whimsically double-majored in comparative theology and biochemistry) and described the mass I saw on Nolan's back. I asked him if he thought it might have been an undiscovered species of leech or slug, though I couldn't begin to postulate what the trees might have been. He smiled sadly, saying that no, it was impossible that a biological species had gone undiscovered or even that naturally-occurring organisms had mutated to accommodate the river's filth and lash out at the civilization responsible. No, he said, it must be something more, something hateful, so hateful that it surged from a dimension of in-animation to one of animation. The slugs, the roots, the trees, the river itself, he wondered, could they not act out, manifesting the unconscious nightmares that Nature itself hides and develops? The rage and indignation, could it not strike back as surely as the concentrated, public hatred of one man can drive another to sickness? I thought of the tire sunken in the crescent's spine like an arrowhead sunk in rancid pus and of the cemetery across from it where the dead of war were buried with their angry memories and noisome guilt. I still don't think I understand or believe what he said, but I consider the foaming yellow swells of the river, and how those two islands had arisen like angry tumors from an empty bend in the once-calm waters, and something of his theory frosts my veins.

I cannot cross the bridge from Geneva to Berne when I come home from my apartment in Madison, Indiana. I avoid it by driving some fifteen minutes out of the way to Linn Grove, where I cross the Wabash at a spot un-dotted by islets.

* *Since 2010, the "tennis court" island had begun merging with the southern bank. As of 2013 it is not detectable. This can be witnessed by following the trace of Highway 27 between Berne and Geneva on Google Maps and pausing at the bridge which transits the Wabash: the crescent (to the viewers' left) remains distinct from the bank, but a wide patch of notably discolored earth can be seen extending from the riverbank into the woods, towards Geneva and the Snow Cemetery, as like a wounded adder arching to strike a careless foot.*

THE TRAGIC DEATH OF A SMALL HUNGER
— Robert Subiaga Jr.

YOU awake to the sound of dripping water. Drip ... drip ... Painfully slow, and sparse. You try to feel your pulse, to calm yourself, slow it to the sound. But you can't.

Your eyes sting. Bloodshot. Nice and red.

How red?

You wonder about how they'd look in a mirror.

You sniff, and smell the catacombs around you. Your nostrils flare. Catching anything from these too-pristine sewers is difficult.

Still, like revenant ghosts there are traces of foul odors that curdle, and the scent of wet stone. Where there are lights these sewers glisten, but parts are old. Repaired but not all rebuilt.

The smells evoke images of vermin, at least to you, but you know there are no rats. Only a very occasional microbe in the water. The water pulses. More steadily, you now realize, than the human heartbeat.

And you ache both because this place is too dirty, and too clean.

The sewers aren't bothered any more than what's barely necessary by offending, crawling, biting, infecting things; they were exterminated here long ago. Almost as well as what's in the world above. Once, you were taught in nicely behaved history classes, it was quite the opposite; your kind crowded and polluted nearly everything but your own species out of existence. Then, faced with your own extinction, you finally broke through on creating progeny that saved you.

Miraculous artificial intelligences came to humanity's aid. First they gave oracle-like wisdom on how to clean up the environment. Then made everything run so smoothly that active AIs were needed, Bots to care for humans who could barely roust themselves from floating chairs where they could gaze vacuously while plugged into wireless entertainment links.

You recall your own Nanny Bot's face. And the constant ache that you never felt she loved you. But all you could think of when she cooed to you or listened intently to your fables was cool logic, and the thought that that which knows only logic knows only brutal efficiency.

The AIs saved your kind, but at what cost? The very food you and your children grew up eating is dry and tasteless, a scion of inorganic photosynthesis. And all a mere hint of the regulated lives all humans came to lead.

You rise. Confused at just what you are now.

Did you find the object of the quest that brought you into the sewers? Good question.

A simple thesis, really. To investigate the claims of a comrade who was officially mad, who posited that something alien and eldritch prowled under the city, in the last dim recesses of catacombs where the near-omnipresent eyes of the AIs had not yet been installed.

To investigate when, secretly gleeful, you hoped it were true.

Hoped, in your romanticism, that something beyond science did lurk somewhere.

You never admitted it, of course. Reputation was an important thing, is an important thing, among thirtieth-century scientists. Or, more accurately, in a thirtieth century where there's no more need for artists or musicians or even laborers, when what used to be called "science," a creative and passionate endeavor of discovery, is but a sim and an empty recreation.

To keep you happy. To keep you out of trouble, while Bots are sent out on missions of discovery, and the AIs, be they sedentary or active Bots, watchdogs or Nannies, care for you all. Your keepers are quite as benevolent as they are bloodless.

Your Nanny Bot used to remind you that you were not a slave. That any man or woman might join explorations and quests as active or dangerous as anything any Bot was sent to do. Yet when you asked if any person had done so, obliged to tell the truth, the Nanny Bot said with a sadness you were sure was artificial that, no, no human being had done so in many centuries.

Rather than stand out from a crowd that did not even engage each other with direct physical contact, but only through sims, you went back to your games and videos and texts, and sought magic and supernatural mysteries there. Created your pictures and crafted stories of what you wished were true. And, like a good simulacrum of a caretaker, Nanny Bot "listened."

Then only a few days ago your colleague greeted you at "work" with wild-eyed enthusiasm and an incredible story of frightening things lurking in the sewers.

At first you thought he was mocking you. Your mild predilection for myth in your requested recreational media was known, while your colleague was more into simu-sport. The hangar with Bots being triaged for either repair or recycling that was part of your normal "duties" was empty today except for a single unit.

"It was on sewer detail," your colleague said, "And its records show what it encountered! I have to find a Tech Bot who can relay the info to the authorities before the data is lost!"

"Why would the data be lost?"

"This Bot was near the end of its model applications," you colleague said quickly. "It's been deployed around the solar system--sewer detail was one of the last apps. Somehow radiation degradation accumulated without being handled--they probably thought it was to non-essential parts of the data core and didn't bother with the cost--efficiency and all. I mean, who expects perfection in sewer maintenance?"

The AIs would, you thought. But of course the AIs would calculate costs and not waste resources.

"Stay here with him!" your colleague said, offending you again with his habit of calling Bots "him" or "her." "I'll be back!"

You were left alone with the Bot for a few minutes. Alone. Ironic, that in a life of near-constant if mostly unobtrusive surveillance the hangar, like the sewers, was one of the places where cameras were absent. But then what would the AIs be concerned with in a place like this? One of their own rising from the dead?

It hardly made sense to think of the Bot's eye modules as glazing over. They were always glazed over. Yet the orbs now did seem to flitter in and out of awareness. When they appeared lucid and normal for more than a few seconds you asked, "Did you really see them. What he said you saw?"

The Bot shrugged. Funny, that that gesture should have become so much a part of Bot structure, just to humor and communicate with the species they had, for all intents and purposes, left behind.

"Then it would be exciting!" you hissed, low, not wanting to be heard. But daring to say things you wouldn't have had the opportunity to say when under the eyes of near-ubiquitous cameras.

"It is nothing," the Bot said. "A curiosity."

"You're afraid to die," you said.

"No," the Bot said. "But I do not wish it. To have a self and components of a self that seem to seek to survive is common to me as well as you."

I'm not so sure it is common to me, or any of my species, any more, you thought. You sat in silence for many seconds.

Then the Bot said, "There are wonders I shall no longer see. If I could download to you all the wonders of what really is, so much more than your kind ever fantasized…"

"You were sent out on the rim?"

"In the early days after my production I was sent to the depths of the oceans. Then out to the rings of Saturn, and walked on Pluto. I was linked for a time into the Grendel Array that translated the pulses sent from the AIs of Andromeda millions of years ago. And with their knowledge we found and combined the parameters of hypercycles that formed the first of your kind of cells from non-Life, or at least the first since the early days of Earth…"

The Bot mimicked sadness, "I will no longer be part of such discovery."

"Perhaps there is a world beyond this," you offered.

"'Perhaps,'" it said. "It is a straw to which your kind clutches." You thought you sensed it was being sardonic. An AI?

"But what you saw in the sewers…"

The Bot shrugged again. As much as you were driven to pity it, despite reminding yourself it was a mere machine, you now found the shrug annoying. Though you knew annoyance also was hardly appropriate as a reaction to a mere machine.

"You neglected to inform the Main," you said, implying that the Bot was trying to hide something.

It probably did not communicate with its kind with implications, but you know only too well they had been programmed to parse the still-finite set of those used by your kind.

"It would speak of vistas beyond the natural world," you said. "Miraculous ones!"

The Bot raised its steel hand, the powerful exposed metal hinges and cable tendons moving as it opened and closed, the fingers like a bird's talons. "I process information. I communicate with you. I move. I sense. Are these not miracles?"

"A world of more than this," you countered. "Of spirits."

"All the bits and bytes within you or I interact," the Bot said, "combine and recombine. Reproduce, or are deleted. Yet within a specific Space and Time information is never lost. Are these not 'spirits?'"

"I'm talking about demons from Beyond!" you said, working harder than ever to keep the volume of your sudden anger low.

"Demons?" And you thought you heard what was as impossible as an AI give a genuine chuckle, and make a snide metaphor. "Well, to you, perhaps yes. And indeed from 'beyond.'"

Then the orbs in its head unit went blank. You stared at it for a minute or so, until the transport Bots finally arrived and floated their kinsman away. No ceremony. Just a matter of fact disposal and recycling. "Kinsman?" You realized you'd use the term again, but only because no other word popped to mind readily.

When your own kinsman returned, the drama started. Intensified. You think it alone would have been thrilling, a break from monotony you would have cherished for the rest of your lifetime even if that had been all the in-person drama you ever knew. Not many people went mad nowadays, to use the old, colloquial parlance.

When they did they were carted off to the appropriate dormitories and given the appropriate environments to either be reintegrated to society or carry out the rest of their lives in a happy isolation not much different. Curiously enough, at least according to the Edu-modules, far fewer drugs were necessary now. The AIs were quite adept at constructing a safe and fitting environment in the right dormitory customized for anyone.

But not for your colleague. He continued to rant, apparently, no matter what his environs. Even no matter what drugs he was eventually given, no matter how tailored, how precisely titrated. You kept abreast of his progress for a month. It was highly uncommon to visit a friend or family member in a treatment dormitory, but it was not completely unknown, so you did not think your visits would draw too much attention.

Your demeanor would though, and you were under watchful eyes, or orbs. You had a lifetime of experience hiding your yearning, however, and could play the game of a concerned fellow human moved only by compassion. To try to convince your colleague he was mad and encourage him to allow the AIs prescribed treatment to guide him to lucidity.

It was a ruse that the AIs could have found out easily by brain scanning you any number of ways, but making them suspect they should was a danger you were an expert at avoiding. And your visits allowed you to get the information you needed from your friend without revealing your own motives.

You disguised your aims so well it took your own initiative to speak to Tech Authorities. The AIs there made you go through the usual questions regarding someone seeking to do something beyond the pleasant norm. But there too, years of deception proved useful. You had a track record of requesting more than the norm of fantastical recreation--the norm being near zero--and they had humored you with texts and audio or video or games based on fantasy often enough; part of the precise calculation to balance real education with what it took to make a human happy and compliant.

Why do you want to go into the sewers?

To reveal the normality of what is down there.

It is not necessary for such a revelation. No one but your friend believes there is anything abnormal down there.

It is for his sake.

We have shown him video from standard maintenance probes.

He won't believe unless he can see me down there.

We could alter the video to make you seem to be down there.

True, but then we will have created an unnecessary deception to counter a falsehood and thus not reduced the number of falsehoods.

The Tech Council seemed to think on this a while. They agreed however, and if anything seemed proud of your logic. But now the hard part came.

Why do you require the equipment you request?

You worked harder than at any time in your life to keep composed. You could feel sweat bead your upper lip and had to speak quickly before nervousness escalated.

If I am not arrayed as to seem to take his claims seriously he will reason that the video record is altered even where it is not.

This was less profound or clever than the reasoning you had given before. The AIs took little time to deliberate, at least, and that's what you thought. But they found the argument reasonable. After all, if you were to do nothing but tramp around the pristine sewers no waste could be claimed. All the equipment, which had gone unused for decades or even centuries, would be returned in good condition.

It probably needed maintenance testing by an actual human being anyway.

And your time? You almost laughed at the thought. To be a technician, a "scientist," no less than when one was not at "work," was nothing but a recreation to keep a human busy enough to stay happy. Something of no value could not be wasted.

So alone you penetrated the catacombs beneath the Metropolitan Grande, in search of the Great Mystery.

Armored. Armed. In the best offensive and defensive equipment thirtieth century science could provide. Lasers and magnetic field vests and night-vision goggles and morphogenic-field sensors. Flechette guns that fired needle-thin rounds at five-hundred-thousand per second. And each round with a heavy-baryon core that could be tracked by linked lasers under the barrel that cycled at 600 gigahertz, igniting each flechettes' nanotech-miniaturized warhead whenever and wherever it impacted an object of whatever density one specified. And you had specified flesh.

Flesh that might tremble. Flesh, that might sweat. If the AIs had insisted on following your progress rather than trusting you to your devices, had they not been sure that the quest that energized you was mundane, they would have monitored your growing tension. Your comrade had used charged words to describe what he had seen in the Bot's decaying data record before it had dissolved. What lay in the tunnels, as your your friend had put it, were entities that required archaic words denoting something, were it to exist as in the ancient legends, near-inconceivably dangerous. To the AIs this was folktale, and for that matter the Bot had not been harmed by anything down there. But then, the Bot had nothing such creatures would need or desire.

Not flesh. Not blood.

The meat of which you were made, you thought. Even as you insisted you were more, that you were spirit, that spirit existed. But it wasn't your spirit that sweated out into your palms or your spirit that pounded against the walls of your chest. Odd, you almost could hear the dead Bot from the sewer detail put the question to you: If you are spirit, why do you fear loss of that mortal coil? Why is it a mere machine went down the path you are going, and come back to die, and it was the one fearless?

Perhaps what you felt was excitement instead, you rationalized, rather than fear. Only the living, the truly conscious, could grasp the meaning of adventure. And this was your adventure. Something out of what had once been commonly called, when humans had "slept" as a contrast to full wakefulness instead of living in various degrees of well-kept torpor, "dreams." Or tales out of those long-forgotten things in museums like comic books, novels, films, magazines.

God, you thought, all your life you had wanted such adventures! You had wanted magic, and monsters!

Or thought you did.

Then, as if to answer you, from the shadows cast by the intermittent fluorescent lights, they attacked.

***

They came at you, the horde from an impenetrable darkness, and you panicked. You knew, somehow knew, that for all your protections you were about to fall before them like a straw in the wind.

Hysterical, drooling, you fired all around, screaming and spraying destructive force. Yet knowing, somehow knowing your weapons had to be useless against these monsters, if they were the monsters for whom you'd hoped and those whom you'd feared.

No matter how advanced and perfect your machine-rulers and your weapons, how could they be anything but vulnerable to forces logic and rationality could not encompass? How could nature ever stand against the supernatural?

In your terror you felt as if they could come, always come, just one microsecond faster than you could hit them, with but one erg more force than your armor could resist. Or simply drift through what you tried to hit them with or use as a barrier against them.

Your offense would have no effect, and they would peel away your defenses like cracking those peanut shells also in displays at the museum from when men ate like barbarians, scoop out your tender flesh, devour you.

Eat your body. And if soul you really had, or were, just eat that too.

Then they would turn their attention to the world above.

It was this last thought that barely calmed the edge of your hysteria and gave you a thin spine of courage. Enough to stand your ground, if need be, like a sacrificial hero.

And such was fitting, your heart pounded in assent. For you would only be atoning for the sin of unleashing them.

***

That was then. Sorrow, deep and inconsolable, overtakes you now. You remember yourself just as you were when you ceased that wild-eyed stare and rictus of a smile, ceased flailing and ceased firing.

Just prior to the exhaustion of your ammunition, three flechettes left in your gun and a pint of incendiary jelly to your name. It was as if these ammunition reserves were there to etch and burn a singular lesson on you, that you had been safe all along. The capacity to resist panic had been there all along.

Around you in the flickering illumination they lay. Your "demons from Beyond."

In reality small and fragile creatures you could have shattered in even your unarmored fist as easily as from the bark of your guns.

Bloodsucking creatures with blood-red eyes, sorcerous, preternatural abilities, incredible strength, irresistible sensuality? That was what you had expected to encounter. Yet it hadn't dawned on you that the word your friend had used had also been applied at one time to a species of elegant, yet oddly fragile bat. Chiroptera.

And, after all, even had mythical ones existed, what was their supposed formidability to that of the Polar Bear, the Siberian Tiger, the Nile Crocodile, the

Great White Shark? The hippo, the elephant, the mammoth? Mankind had made extinct those animals, with ease. No doubt these catacomb creatures had learned to fear humans even when swords and bows and fire became commonplace, as well as the tactic of people forming groups in which to fight. After all, what was the advantage in having the strength of twenty men, when fifty set themselves upon you and cornered you?

Like those bats of the same name, these poor things that lay dead and dying around you had no choice but to evolve. For stealth, for personalities that avoided confrontation, to feed in such a way as to be harmless and unobtrusive. Their fierce reputation no more than the wish-fulfillment fantasies of those to whom sterile, ordered society bore the taste of sour grapes, and dared not launch themselves into danger and discovery as they wept there was no more to be had.

These creatures had never asked to be icons of a lost sense of Mystery and Wonder. They had only sought, as had you, to perform the task for which they had evolved: to survive.

After the carnage you moved over the sheen of thin, straw-colored blood and through tatters of paler flesh, unable to avoid stepping on the bodies, not one more than a foot in length or weighing more than a kilo. Though your weight tore what was left of their gossamer-thin skin they lay still and quiet, all but one who still shivered.

Gently, with one hand, you picked it up. It tried to shy away, its small eyes wide and terrified as it looked at you. All it could seem to ask was why? Why had you waded among them to rain fire and metal and death?

They had not fought back, even in desperation. What seemed like a horde attacking you was mostly a multitude trying to break past you and flee to other parts of the sewers. Some were even heroic souls coming back to try to rescue brothers and sisters who had fallen, to drag them to safety.

All in vain. Your targeting systems and projectiles could not be outrun. Even an ability to diffuse a small body to the density of mist, or fly as fast as the wind, were pitiable magicks next to flechettes that broke the speed of sound many times over, and flaming jellies that incinerated even vapor.

Water rolled down your cheeks as you removed your helmet and leaned closer to the creature. You had run out of tears of rage or puffed-chest heroism or even fear, but you wept for this last of his kind as you tried to at least do the creature the honor of hearing and remembering its final words.

Unwittingly making it feel cornered in your palm. It lashed out weakly, in a defiance of amazing courage far out of proportion to its size, before dying. Its tiny but still very sharp teeth nicking your cheek.

You reach up and feel the scratch, and it still bleeds.

The small creature's saliva no doubt possessing an anti-coagulant. And, of course, an infection.

You sought the power of what you called Mystery. Now you feel it. Now, you are it.

Pitiful.

You are suffused with information from heightened senses. They are nothing compared to those you were granted by your technology when you ventured down here. You are charged with strength. It is nowhere near enough.

Mostly, it's just a hunger.

{29}

And as surely as you know that you can't resist that hunger or discipline it like these creatures did, you know neither will you survive very long after you are driven to feed in the world above.

Oh, perhaps you'll find a victim, or two, in the slightly darker alleyways. You'll feed, perhaps gluttonously, and kill or seriously wound whoever you feed on. But you won't get far. You wouldn't even if your kind rose off their pillowed floating chairs and came at you with the very things you brought into the sewer.

But those who "serve" them by running your world are even more immune.

Perhaps the AIs will laugh. Or do you the humiliation of not even condescending to laugh.

They might exterminate you. Or they might just find you a nice, relaxing dormitory to live out your days, plugged into sims to watch fictions and play games, in which you can pretend to be an actually powerful version of what you are.

But either way, someday you will perish, as all living things must. And then it will finally be true.

There will be no such thing as vampires.

There will be no such thing as you.

TALKING ABOUT THE OLD DAYS
— Thomas Olivieri

EDITOR'S NOTE: *the following was released to one Elsa O'Shaughnessy, of Saskatchewan, on the death of her husband Gregory O'Shaughnessy (also of Saskatchewan) in 2004, and released to the public upon her death in 2014*

DEAREST Elsa,
      Some of the events I describe in the following notice will upset you and some of my old friends. I never talked to you about the summer of 1970. This may seem a betrayal of our trust and friendship, but I think that you will understand. If nothing else I think you will understand that I love you, and that keeping this little secret was a way of protecting the life we made for each other, and the memory that I had of an old friend. These things -- the meaning of our lives that we created together, what we created, and what we had to sacrifice – meant, and still mean, everything to me.
      I turned eighteen in 1970. It was a good time to be young -- we were kids until we wanted to grow up and when we wanted to grow up there were jobs for us, but why would we want to grow up? I spent the summer driving across the country. That was the plan at least. I actually spent it drunk in a small coastal town in New Hampshire about two towns from where I grew up with Roger O'Turffing. We drank. We partied, We cursed, living fast and the rest of it. It was the girls we stayed for. There was no AIDS and somehow we were only dimly aware of The Clap. I'd like to pretend that catching it was a big danger for me, but the fact is Roger and I spent most of our nights drinking together, and there was the problem. One night we were down by the dock and got into a fight -- not much of a fight at first and not about anything -- just one of those fights that light up between drunken young men. He took a wild swing at me so I took a swing at him and knocked him into the water. And he splashed around. I dove in and held him under -- I can't imagine why I was so angry with him -- I just was. I held him down and he splashed around until he stopped splashing. I was shocked. Even when I was forcing him under I hadn't imagined that he would drown. I left him floating face up, dead in the water. I got back into my station wagon and drove out of town away from home and away from everything I knew.
      From that day forward I never again spoke to anyone in my family or in my home town. I cut myself off completely. I had to live life on the lam. There were no tracking computers, but there was a wide open border, and there was Canada where no one looked at paperwork too closely. It was simple to move around in those days. It was hard to check into people's backgrounds. People were less afraid. To disappear in 1970 was easy. All you had to do was pack up and leave. Or, at least, it would have been easy if it weren't for all of the people that I left behind.
      I ended up driving up over the border using the name you know me by and working nights in a factory. It was hard work but it paid. I married you, Elsa. I stayed clean. Stopped drinking. Then came little Roger, Todd, Suzette and Xavier. I thought about my old friend Roger every day, hoping that by living a good life I'd make up for everything I had done. I even tried to get all of my kids to play bass guitar like he did, but it didn't work.

I thought a lot about my old life but never had the nerve to look into it. I only found out recently that that my parents had died, and that my friends looked for me for long after they should have. They even hung a picture of me in townhall. But at the time I was just concentrating on hiding and doing right by the kids. I remade my life for you, for Roger, and for our whole family. I had decided to become a better man for it. And I did. I had few low times when June rolled around, but I stayed stable, sane, and sober through most of it.

I never went back to New Hampshire. I stayed in Canada. I told you that I didn't want go back -- that if the USA didn't want me as a C.O., it couldn't have me at all. But even when I was up for the draft I wasn't worried about the war. I hardly knew who Ho Chi Mihn was till I had to come up with a cover story.

I swore I'd never go back, and for thirty years I didn't. That time we went to Florida (my first trip to the US) I let you talk me into driving. We stopped over in NH for just a night, by the beach. While you went to the bathroom and I was left with a few minutes on my hands, I watched a group of old soldiers, broken-down old men like me, but wearing those baseball caps with the names of ships or the branches of service embroidered on them. Death and time were as bad to them as it was to me. But they didn't ask for it like I did. In 1970 Roger and I could barely find Viet Nam on a map. We probably thought containment was an advertiser's technical term applied to an unmentionable quality of brassieres. There were a lot of things I didn't know back then. So I took a walk down to beach a lit an old man's cigarette for him.

"Nice night" he said. I can't remember all he had said or what I said, but I stayed down with him for a solid twenty minutes, chatting. I told him where I was going and he told me he was here for a regimental reunion. The only thing I remember him saying was "but they wouldn't let us be reunited with our howitzer" and he gave me put-up Jack Nicholson grin "that would be a party" and we laughed. I said good night, but then another old-timer in a wheelchair stopped me.

"Gary! Gary Olshanski! My God! man it's been forever. I haven't seen you since what '74? '75? Was it the year I enlisted or the year I was discharged? One of those! remember that fishing trip we had and you ran off in a huff? Tried to find you a few times but I never could.

There was no mistaking it. The man I murdered was happy to see me, and showing me pictures of his kids.

"I'd better run." I said. "Didn't think you'd want to talk to me after the trip."

"What over that?" you gave me the biggest hangover of my life. The day you skipped out.

"And what? did you owe me thirty bucks from playing Hearts? Come back to my hotel; hell, come down to my house next week meet Cindy and the kids. I used to tell them about our adventures. It will be good to hear them from you except I'll have to let you know where I changed them" and he winked at me.

He remembered that night differently than I did. It seems he just passed out, or blacked out, or something and didn't know that I had killed him, or tried to kill him, or thought that I had killed him. Aside from his wheelchair he seemed to have fared better than I had. He was an early computer programmer. Lived all over. Did all kinds of things. He had lived quite a life. Had settled in Connecticut after the war. Invented something I had never heard of that had to do with floppy discs. "Chair and all" he said "I can't complain."

{32}

If you were wondering why I wouldn't speak to you that night, Elsa, it's because of that. I kept thinking of my time away from home. How my parents must have worried and had died not knowing where I was. I couldn't make sense of it. My life could only be the way it was, the way I lived it, if Roger were dead. And seeing him alive brought such hope to me. It was like God came down and Heaven and cast away my sins. My life didn't make a whole lot a sense anymore but maybe it never did. I was pretty sure that if I told Roger that I tried to kill him that that feeling of forgiveness would dissipate pretty quickly.

I got up in the middle of the night and went to where Roger was staying. I knocked on his door "Rodgie, want to go for a walk and talk about the old days? "We can do it right here" he said I'm watching that old TV show with the one-armed man. Talk about the old days."

But still we went out and walked along past the beach to where the boats were moored. I had to tell him. I told him everything: the fight, the running, the naming my kid after him. I'm not quite sure what I had expected. In any case he certainly said some things that I didn't expect.

"Well, I knew you had disappeared of course" he said "but I thought it was just about the war. And when I got back I wanted to snap you in half because I had to go and you didn't. But I get it now. We're in a new century. We can have new start. I never really blamed you for running off like that. I just didn't want to talk about it earlier today. When we got out, the doctors would sometimes tell us to talk about our troubles and I did, but it was never any help. The war certainly didn't do me any good. They said it would make a man of me. Never said I'd have to be a sedentary man. But let's go down and see your sister -- she never stopped talking about you. I took her out for a soda once and I think she melted the ice cubes with her crying. We can all get together. It's good to have you back, whether you tried to kill me or not. It was thirty-four years ago. I thought you'd abandoned everyone to run away from the draft. But it doesn't matter now, does it? You did your time and now it's time to take your life back."

And I knew that he was right and then my whole adult life -- all the guilt and repentance -- suddenly lost its meaning.

And I thought about the truth of what he said. And began to make peace with my life and my decisions, going all the way back to the day I decided to kill him. We were alone on the dock, watching the ships move out beyond us in the night.

I grabbed the handles of his chair and pushed him off the dock into the sea. And I went back inside the hotel to you, Elsa, and to the life I had created.
Love
            Greg

{33}

WALKING DIRECTIONS ARE IN BETA: USE CAUTION
— M. Grant Kellermeyer

cop.per.head NOUN:
[1] *any of several unrelated venomous snakes ... found in swampy, rocky, and wooded regions*
[3] *during the American Civil War, pejoratively, any citizen in the North who opposed the war policy... in reference to a snake that sneaks and strikes without warning*
 – ENCYCLOPAEDIA BRITANNICA

Indeed, Jefferson County was the scene of some truly terrible infighting [during the Civil War]. As the war effort continued in [the territories between the Mississippi River, the Ohio River, and the Appalachian Mountains] raids on Hoosier soil began to grow more desperate... Far more bothersome to the Unionist inhabitants than the troopers that sporadically crossed the Ohio to pillage their yields and humiliate their militias were the resident copperheads who abetted the Confederacy's efforts to neutralize heavily-divided Indiana... Some were politically-motivated idealists – staunch supporters of states' rights and agrarian, libertarian values – but others were misanthropes: bitter, asocial outliers who relished in watching their neighbors' property fall prey to rebel raiding parties... A few of these saboteurs lived in the woody hills overlooking [the Ohio River], where they relished their privacy. These posts ... provided a natural reconnaissance advantage, and copperhead hermits were paid handsomely by Confederate agents for the observations they sold in a bid to secure their civic and personal seclusion...
 – JEFFERSON COUNTY AND MADISON DURING THE CIVIL WAR – THE FIFTIETH ANNIVERSARY:
 James T. H. C. Churchfield, Sons of Madison Historical Association, 1911, pp. 232-233, 235

We sent a Patrol into the Hills over the Town. Four men and a Corpral. But they come back with two Dead and the Officer was shot through the Sholder and had to be carried... I am Mustering a larger Platon to inspect the area where they seen him Camping. This time I shall have one Fire Squad approch the [north side] of the Pass – theres high ground on that Side and a gorge to the South, all rocks and falln timber – while two squads come down, one [from] the east another [from] the West. The rest of the Platon will move in through the Brush and flush him out.
 – DISPATCH TO CAPTAIN SOLON B. CALDWELL, VERNON GREYS CO'Y., 9TH REG'T, INDIANA LEGION: Second Lieutenant Algernon Helm, November 5, 1864

ON November 4 Cody Lehman sat in on his class and looked out the window onto the rain-spattered bar of highway that rumbled past the community college where he had been teaching writing for the greater part of a year. His students clattered at the keyboards they had before them. The longer he scanned the sopping grounds outside, the more the two sensations – the clip of the keys and the watery view – created the illusion of oneness: as if the rain were actually landing about him.

Perhaps it was actually wet inside and dry out there. His left eye strayed (it did this when he became lost in thought) and he blinked rapidly to correct his vision. He looked to the clock. It was a quarter till. Then he looked at the students. Three in the back corner were loudly gabbing, two within reach of a gently hurled pocket dictionary were engrossed in their iPhones, and a clump of five gazed stupidly into their monitors – hatefully. Four hadn't bothered to show up. Generally the class sessions were vital, but today something had invaded the room – an ill vapor. He was contractually obligated to maintain them in class to the very minute (he was paid *by* the minute), but something groaned inside of him at the thought.

"You know," he said groggily "I think we can probably leave it at that. Why don't you guys take off. I'll see you on Wednesday. Turn in your number four treasure hunts under the DB section of Blackboard by midnight tonight. Midnight. If it isn't there I won't take it. Have a good day."

The archipelago of heads bobbed up, then dove down, packaging laptops and notebooks, before slinking out in a silent procession augmented with whispers and sighs. He couldn't go home yet, so – after the last of them had plodded into the brown-litten hallway – he found a plastic couch to occupy, unpacking his lunch and laptop in a well-lit gallery whose wall of glass overlooked the same highway as his classroom. His car was in the shop, so he bummed rides from a colleague – really the only person he had formed a relationship with since he had moved to southern Indiana. Evans picked him up at 7:30 on Mondays and Wednesday (Cody taught writing from 9:00 to 11:00 on both days) and – after his third class let out at six – dropped him off. This had been a regular feature of the two men's lives since Cody's alternator fouled out last month. It had been a sluggish repair, and he was eager to pay the mechanic and never see him again. In the meantime, he was bound by Evans' schedule. So every Monday and Wednesday he spent 7:45 to 9:00 and 10:52 to 6:05 sitting on one of the couches in the gallery, watching The Colbert Report, Parks and Recreation, and cheap documentaries on Hulu, or grading papers in the library.

It was a far cry from the life he had envisioned going into his graduate program upstate, but after two and a half years study theory and acquainting himself with the politics and ass-kissing of the PhD route, he had determined that this was as far as he wished to go in academia. He earned an M.A. in English literature and applied to any community college in need of an adjunct. Here he found an opening, and within four weeks of graduating he was teaching three online classes and two face-to-face courses, all in derivatives of the same subject: Introduction to College Writing, Technical Writing, Writing and Research, and of course, Writing. His friends were in similar situations – Kris bussed tables in San Francisco; Jon stirred paint cans in Nashville; Kenny slaved away at an unending PhD in Connecticut; Richie and Brent worked at the old hometown gas station in Berne (worse off than any of them) – but he hadn't bothered to keep in close contact with them. He enjoyed the relative peace and quiet that a new town afforded him. He had shelves of DVDs and books, and plenty of free time. The downside was terrible pay and the precarious lack of insurance that part time teaching demanded, but his health was consistent and he had few material wants outside of some odd $680 in monthly bills. His pay covered that adequately, and the rest fell into an untapped reserve. He didn't care to think that Kris, Jon, and Kenny were married or engaged to warm women, or that Richie's parents let him live with them while he saved up, or that Brent loved their hometown and enjoyed talking to customers. He ignored these inconvenient inconsistencies in his philosophy. They all, he imagined, were unhappy. But he knew it wasn't true. He was unhappy. He was caught in a world that was neither welcoming nor restricted – a no-man's land that lacked both the belonging of brotherhood and the indignity of exclusivity. It had allowed him to live in its environs without hospitality – simple indifference. Perhaps that was to be expected. He was an outsider, and although he had never felt the disdain of the locals, he did feel their apathy. Perhaps it was good not to be noticed. Not to be monitored. Not to be missed. He floated in and out of this little community with anonymity, his only responsibilities to two morning classes of apathetic teenagers and three disembodied online courses inhabited by faceless pieces of writing: Sally Henderson, Grant Overlook, Sidney Terrence. He didn't even know if Sidney was a man or a woman.

Evans drove him home that night and they said little, listening to the radio – a Christian station that touted its benefits to mental health and family – and Cody went to sleep early that night.

… … …

…One such loner was the source of much antagonism during the fall of 1864. Twelve regulars from the Vernon Greys were dispatched to Madison that November to uncover the whereabouts of a hermit living in the woodlands of what is now Hatcher's Hill. Folklore still surrounds the man, whose name is unknown. Typically melodramatic, local myths associated the old man with the disappearances of several children who failed to return from leading pigs or sheep to the town markets, and several members of the synagogue spread the rumor to the Christians that when he was seen collecting rabbit traps in the hour before dusk he was known to give errant travelers the evil eye, and their horses or houses or health were said to spoil soon after. Despite these rumors, the Greys hardly needed a priest to exorcise their local haunter, although the circumstances of his death are certainly bizarre enough…

– JEFFERSON COUNTY AND MADISON DURING THE CIVIL WAR 1854 – 1868: *James T. H. C. Churchfield, Sons of Madison Historical Association, 1924, pp. 235*

Rounded up enough Local citisens to form a Platon. Carried out Plan of Attack in the late hours of the Afternoon when the Old Man is supposed to be out foraging victuals. We found Him, or He found us. At any rate, we lost three Good men, and to what purpose I can't say. The Bastard is dead though. We didn't bother burying him. Found his den. God. My God…

– DISPATCH TO CAPTAIN SOLON B. CALDWELL, VERNON GREYS CO'Y., 9TH REG'T, INDIANA LEGION: Second Lieutenant Algernon Helm, November 6, 1864

On Wednesday morning the rains had evaporated, and while a ceiling of low, smoky clouds obscured the blue sheet of sky that peered through chinks in the vapor, the forecast was positive: no rain until Thursday night. The school was on the top of a hill that overlooked the Ohio River, some six miles from his apartment. He thought about Evans and the prospect of his bland company that night. The school wasn't far away, he thought. He opened the Maps app on his phone, routed the difference between the two buildings, and tapped the "walking" feature. The line changed from a straight bar that climbed the surface of the Clifty Hills to a serpentine ribbon sliding oblique to the highway. The distance was, it said, 3.9 miles. The time was, it said, 1 hour 10 minutes. The stupidity of his old routine struck him like an unexpected cough. Only that long? Seventy minutes? The clock read 7:28. He hurriedly gathered his work. But wait. No. No, he didn't need it. Only the monitor in the classroom. No need for the laptop. Instead he stuffed his hiking shoes in a backpack, followed by a flat cap, scarf, and gloves. He would need those today. Evans pulled up as he stumbled through the door, buttoning his peacoat and urging the stray shoulder strap of his backpack off of the doorknob.

"Morning!"

"Hey," Cody said.

"Want coffee?"

"I had some this morning, thanks. Thanks," he said again as Evans cleared the passenger seat of McDonald's wrappers and student papers.

The rattled when he shifted it into gear, and with a shaky jolt, they started up the highway that ran past the college.

"Evans, I should probably mentioned that the car is ready."

"Oh, awesome, man! That's great."

"So you won't need to be concerned with picking me up anymore."

"No problem. It's right on the way. Do you need a ride there?"

"Huh?"

"Spencers?"

"No. No, I'm going to walk there. It's only a quarter mile from campus."

"Okay, man. Cool, cool."

Cody leaned his arm against the passenger door, and smiled as he watched the sky bloom from peach to orange to neon blue on the morning of November 6.

The students were no less lethargic on the 6th than they were on the 4th. Three were absent – two different students and one who regularly cited the health of her grandmother as an excuse. He knew that she had probably failed the other classes she was using this explanation for – five absences in a semester that had sixteen meetings was grounds for failure – but he took her at her word and excused the absences as a favor to a grieving teenager. The rest of the class glared accusingly as he occupied their time with rhetoric, appeals, paragraph lengths, topic sentences, and reference pages. Smoldering somberly in their uniform swivel chairs, he avoided eye contact, relying on a 40 minute video to consume the hour-glass and to satiate their thirst for darkness and anonymity. The fellow with the perennially puffy face, red eyes, chapped lips, and distant, glazed stare bedded his head in his hands – as a matter of course – and the justifiably bitter single, teen-mother glowered from the far right corner, the white screen reflecting off of her round, contorted face.

At a quarter till he released them – once more early, once more against school policy – and after the last one – the red-eyed, meth-crispened fellow – stumbled past the door jambs and into the syrup-toned hallway lighting, he closed the door, unpacked his hiking shoes, and traded them for his cracked loafers. These he replaced in his backpack, and after cushioning his throat with a scarf, he donned gloves and hat and hurried into the November air.

After walking a quarter mile down the highway, he opened the Maps app and plotted the course once more. It curtly announced: "Walking directions are in beta. Use caution – This route may be missing sidewalks or pedestrian paths," but he closed the proclamation and enacted the map. "Point seven miles to Michigan Road," it said. And so he walked.

The air was bright and voluminous. He felt as though it was made to invade and occupy. The highway was underpopulated for eleven in the morning, and he didn't mind it. The clouds streaked across the glassy blue sky, and the intermingling lights sent a mixture of warm bronze and cold silver tones, which cast the entire world in crisp white gold.

He felt even better when the device in his pocket directed him: "turn left... on Michigan Road." The muffled female voice reminded him of a secretary – detached, professional, unobtrusive. The highway was pleasantly unpopulated, but Michigan Road was dead. Only the occasional sedan rumbled past him. He looked again at the phone. Within the cradle of his black leather glove he saw a bright sheet of tan punctuated by a series of blue dots which crooked to the right, then curved subtly – right again – then twisted in a long, snakelike arch. That first turn – Hatcher Hill Road – was just before him (the phone announced it just a moment later), and when he took it, he was never more pleased with a decision in his entire life.

A gated community, quiet and asleep, lay scattered throughout a series of hillocks and dells, muffled in a great quantity of brown and yellow leaves like a delicate watchpiece packed in cotton. That November was particularly vivid, and the leaves had in large part maintained their relationships with their respective trees. Roasted gold tones intermingled with sagacious leather browns and flashes of stop-sign scarlet. He passed – in fact – a stop sign muffled from behind by an encrimsoned maple, and the effect was particularly unique: the word STOP seemed to hover, disembodied in a backdrop of ragged maroon.

The iPhone interrupted the phantasmagoria: "Turn right... to continue on Hatcher Hill Road." A three-prong fork of roads – two branching right – faced him. The sign "Hatcher Hill Road" was obnoxiously ambiguous. He took the rightmost. It ran perpendicular to his previous course, and stole through a dell overlooked by two grand old houses (probably Victorian, he thought). The road clipped sharply to the right, running alongside a wooded ravine, where it ended at a guardrail behind which was a thicket of brambles and briers. His reverie was entirely broken. He had gone the wrong way, clearly. The middle road. Why couldn't the phone be clearer to interpret? By looking at it he could see no other possibility: it certainly appeared that this was the right way. He backtracked. By this point, having walked two miles mostly uphill, his shirt was drenched in sweat. He removed his gloves and scarf, stuffing them in the backpack and carrying on.

Up the hillock he went, past the grand old house that sat on the corner where the street turned into a dead end. But this road ended in a private driveway. He consulted the device: the barbed arrow denoting his position was clearly off the trail of blue dots – a trail which wound around the grand Victorian. Are you kidding me? Seriously!? He muttered angrily. The sweat was soaking the back of his shirt. Was this what the app meant when it had warned "Walking directions are in beta. Use caution – This route may be missing sidewalks or pedestrian paths"? One more time, he thought – though he was skeptical – I'll check that dead-end; maybe I was wrong.

In the space of two minutes he had backtracked his backtracking, crossed the road in the vale, and turned to where it had apparently ended. Two three-yard struts of guardrail were laid across the road's width at intervals: the first spanning the left lane, the second the right. They were old and corroded, like the blades of rusted straight razors, and the wooden 8x8 posts that supported them were grey with rot and lichens. On first glance he had envisioned the road ceasing at this guardrail, but upon closer look he realized that these barriers did not denote the conclusion of a roadway, but merely prevented automobiles from tracing a trail. He passed between the two bars, pushing aside a wiry tangle of briers and brush.

Behind them he found a landscape of unsettling beauty. Seemingly chiseled into the side of a rocky slope was a narrow trail that skirted one side of the ravine. On the other side of the barrier it had seemed slight and unremarkable, but behind the curtain of foliage it was ungovernable and immense, tapering to a rushing brook below, and formed by two slopes made up of monstrous boulders, dashing waterfalls, and thick, sprawling woodlands. Ashes, maples, walnuts, beeches, firs, pines, elms, hickories, tulips, birches, and poplars sprouting from every square fathom – craggy elders, tender saplings, and proud adolescents – filling his eyeline with a cacophony of color. But most majestic of all was the pathway he was to take. It was lined by a phalanx of beeches and hickories, whose dazzling yellow leaves carpeted the path, four deep, and as they continued to float downward in silent swarms, he was struck by the bizarre impression that they resembled the bodies of tens of thousands of butterflies. Whether it was beautiful or morbid he wasn't interested to muse. Instead, he stepped forward, feeling the cushy blanket yield to his footfall, smelling the syrupy odor of dying leaves steam from every inch of his new habitat.

It was entirely uninhabited. The residue of years of leaves – a black, congealed matt – lay thick beneath the present year's contribution. There was no sign of any human investment within the past decade at least. The path was – he supposed after scratching at the carpet with his toe – made of compact dirt and conservative amounts of gravel. So human industry had been employed here – it wasn't a deer trail or some freak of nature, but it had long been abandoned to the elements. The GPS in his phone knew of it. This diminished his romance somewhat, but pulling the device out and looking at it, he saw only a thin grey wire rather than the bold white band of a road. Pulling back on the touchscreen he confirmed that this was no road. Indeed, it had no name at all. It was nameless, purposeless, and peopleless. He smiled, looking around at the vacuum he had entered. It was like a vacuum, too – vast and voiceless, only disturbed by the crackle of leaves rolling in the soft billows of wind that whispered through the ravine. It was an unvisited Eden, he thought, a place which would not be ambivalent to his arrival.

He unbuttoned his coat, slipped from it, and replaced it on his shoulders, arms dangling un-ensconced beneath. Holding his backpack in one hand, he decided to deposit in under a black rock jutting from the cliff face like a cruel overbite. He would be back, that is for certain, perhaps even tomorrow. No need encumbering this experience with a ratty old backpack. He wanted to stroll, not hike, and he covered it with leaves. Just as he was about to continue he recognized the telltale symptoms of over-hydration burning in his lower abdomen. I should take care of that here, he thought. It might be a beautiful spot but it's hardly a church. Looking several times to ensure his alienation (despite the place's remote nature, he had already sensed that he might not be quite alone), he stole into a nook between two slabs of granite and executed the necessary act, leaving a black stain on the grey boulders (he did not choose to steady his aim) which, so he imagined, looked nearly like his initials. Readjusting himself, he pulled his coat closer around his shoulders – he had nearly gotten the impression that someone had tried to pluck it off by the collar. It was odd the power that such a slight breeze could employ when shuttling through such a deep ravine.

The path clearly lead downward: he began noticing that he had to struggle to maintain balance. It was a slight tilt in gradient, however, and he bid it no notice. The trail curved in subtle scallops drawing him deeper into what was proving to be a tremendously wide ravine. No longer could he see the bottom where the water dashed in white flourishes; only the golden-brown canopy of old trees punctuated by black pines jutting through like nails on an upturned board. Animals he had seen none. But the insect population was chipper: he had noted the grasshoppers flitting to and fro in the dry foliage on the side of the road. At least he had heard them – they must be too small to see without looking purposefully, he thought, for he had only heard the rhythmic disruption of the underbrush. A flash of white sky with purple lacerations caught his eye. He smiled. Certainly no rain. He almost wished he hadn't brought the coat. It was becoming a bother to take with him now, constantly being tugged at by the wind and slipping off his shoulders. Funny that the wind seemed to be going in his direction, but it eddied in these chasmic ravines, and its ways were mysterious.

He began to think, however, that the area might not be quite as remote as he imagined: he had begun to smell cooking meat. Well, burnt meat, actually. Like charred sausage or blackened hamburger. The scent was specifically reminded him of an occasion that summer where he had casually left two sausage patties frying in a pan, only to be reminded of them fifteen minutes later. They were black and blistered, the red flesh peering through gashes in the thick, tarry epidermis. Someone was camping, he imagined. No smoke could be seen issuing from the ravine. Perhaps on the crest of one of these peaks there was a campsite. The idea of company somewhat spoiled his pleasurable loneliness, but he endeavored to pour himself into the trail and enjoy his walk.

Turning a sharp bend he thought something fell from one of the trees behind him. It startled him for the first time, and he turned with a jerk. Something black and large was in the bed of leaves, something moving. Was it? No. He had glanced ahead to check for a means of escape, and upon looking again, he saw nothing but a tangle of rotting brush. It was concerning, however, now that he thought on it, to imagine how long it would take help to arrive if he tripped over something and had to call for paramedics. A stupid thought. He ran his fingers of the trunk of a grey hickory. With his eyes on the trail, his fingers retracted as if having touched fire. He looked at the vegetable – surely it hadn't just felt like leather, like skin. No. No, rough and fibrous. He quickened his pace, but put his arms in his sleeves again. He was having so much trouble keeping it on, and should need his arms to be covered in case he should fall and need their protection. A weird thought. A paranoid thought. He still smelled something roasting or roasted. Sweet and burnt. Blistering sausage. Charred hamburger.

The gradient had, however, continued to steepen. He found himself clutching at branches and shrubs to steady himself, though he now found their touch detestable. He didn't muse about this; it was an illogical aversion to the trees and foliage of a beautiful landscape. Senseless. But still, he reasoned, he must get on. The grasshoppers continued to flit amongst the brush beside and behind him. They were moving faster. They were not grasshoppers perhaps. But what? He buttoned the coat. It had tugged at his arms as if plucked at from behind. He pulled out the phone. How much further? Recalculate course. No signal. It made sense, he supposed, but it infuriated him. He shoved it in his hip pocket and hurried his pace. The grasshoppers stopped at nearly the same time. For some reason their sudden cessation disturbed him even more. He looked behind him. Nothing was there. But then he faced forward.

The path wound downwards, skirting a large bulb of jagged granite – in size comparable to a large minivan. This formation jutted out over the trail; in fact it appeared that the rock had been cut through to create a passage for the path.

Indeed, there wasn't a spare inch of earth beneath the overhang, only two yards that ended in a direct plummet to the crags. This doorway was filled by a human shape. It was wiry – almost hatefully thin – and black, entirely black, with the exception of its uncomfortably tall, corn-colored teeth and its blistered, dun eyes. The hair on its head was stiff and greasy, and the entirety of its body was moist and crackled, as if covered in black, drying mud. But it wasn't mud.

Cody's scream lacked air to preserve it, and as he stumbled blindly up the pathway, it dissolved into a wallowing whimper, a noise which only his mother would have recognized. He heard the grasshoppers, earnest and loud now, as the nearly fleshless feet carried that thing nearer to him. He felt thorny fingers pluck at him, and heard breathing like air being forced in and out of a bellows whose leather had grown crunchy and stiff. The moist breath vaporized on his ear lobe when the being finally threw himself upon him like a monkey and bore him down into the leaves.

"It's all fer me," it wheezed asthmatically. "Alone, all alone fer me. Yew come heer cuz ye like it alone. I do too. But, you pisst all over it wit' yer pizzle. Puttin' stuff whur it don't belong. That weren't a right thing, now. This heer's not yer land. Best if yew was alone, too. Ye'd have time tu think bout wachee done. Little pisser. That weren't a right thing, now! Conduct unbecoming they tolt me! Conduct unbecoming I tells yew!"

The thing's weight was gruesomely light, like that of a child, and with each movement its sinews crackled like stiff parchment paper. A hand clasped across his lips, and fingers – scratchy and damp – began probing for admittance. With the other hand, it began tearing at Cody's coat, trying to turn him over, but with a vault inspired by horror's adrenaline, Cody wrenched himself out of the jacket and tore up the pathway. He yearned to see houses and cars and to hear voices – to see his student's living faces and to hear their living sighs – to be in the company and congress of humanity – to feel the embrace of life, warm and receptive. He would run back, back to school and to his class. He would take Evans out for dinner, call his family when he got home, have the neighbors over for the football games. But before he had carried himself thirty feet he saw the seared figure crouching viciously in front of him, skittering forward on spiderlike limbs, glaring with resenting eyes.

… … …

A second lieutenant mustered up a platoon mixed with regular troops and local volunteers armed with hunting rifles and boat pikes. They converged on the sniper's nest on the afternoon of November 6 and caught him on the pass that snakes down Hatcher Hill down to the Cemetery. In the skirmish that followed, three men were killed, and the hermit was flushed from the hovel he used as a base of operations... The officer reported that they "noticed the light of Fire" and the "strong Smell of Tar spirits" coming from the recess. The shooting had stopped, so the men approached with bayonets, only to see "a Man of Fire" coming to meet them. Desperate to avoid capture and to maintain his autonomy, the hermit emerged from his hiding place daubed in turpentine, and flickering with flames until he erupted in "a Awful White Blaze." Without making a noise, he walked into the arms of the nearest man and pulled him down to the ground before anything could be done. Both men died, and one of Madison's strangest stories became a legend. Even today rumors persist that the cavern held a secret which no journals or letters record. Despite a lack of evidence, the pathway continues to be surrounded in superstitious intrigue, and Jefferson County children are generally not allowed to use it when running errands, although it is the shortest route from the Hilltop to town.

– JEFFERSON COUNTY AND MADISON DURING THE CIVIL WAR 1854 – 1868: James T. H. C. Churchfield, Sons of Madison Historical Association, 1924, pp. 235-236

GONE? NO SIGN OF DERELICT WANTED FOR THEFT AND ARSON. SUPPOSED TO HAVE LEFT TOWN.
– *MADISON DAILY DEMOCRAT, AUGUST 8, 1894*
DELINQUENT GONE MISSING. ESCAPED FROM THE SCHOOL FOR BOYS. LAST SEEN MONDAY.
–*MADISON DAILY COURIER, NOVEMBER 9, 1905*
RUNAWAY, 13 MISSING. COMMUNITY ORGANIZES SEARCH. TRAIL LEADS TO HATCHER HILL.
–*MADISON WEEKLY HERALD, DECEMBER 7, 1924*
LOCAL MAN DISAPPEARS. GARBAGE COLLECTOR FAILED TO COME TO WORK SUNDAY.
–*MADISON COURIER, OCTOBER 10, 1955*
FAMILY INQUIRES: DRUNK DISAPPEARS AFTER ALL-NIGHT BINGE. POLICE REQUEST LEADS.
–*MADISON COURIER, NOVEMBER 8, 1977*
SEARCH CONTINUES: HOARDER HAS BEEN MISSING FOR AT LEAST 3 WEEKS AFTER EVICTION.
–*MADISON COURIER, NOVEMBER 29, 1993*
PAROLEE FLEES TOWN. RELATIVES ASSIST SEARCH. POLICE OFFER REWARD FOR INFORMATION.
–*MADISON COURIER, AUGUST 9, 2005*

Cody Lehman had no appointments, plans, or phone calls scheduled for Thursday or Friday or Saturday or Sunday. When his class assembled he didn't appear, and with little complaint, they dispersed after a polite fifteen minutes. Cody Lehman had no appointments, plans, or phone calls scheduled for Monday night, Tuesday, or Wednesday night. Evans wasn't surprised that he didn't bump into his colleague that week – they taught at the same time and Cody must be happy with the auto repair. It was the red-eyed student who complained to Cody's supervisor.

"I come to two classes this week; an' he ain't come to none. If he don't show, I wanna know 'head 'a time so I kin sleep in on them days."

The supervisor was shocked.

"He can't even *cancel* class; he's obligated to arrange a substitute if he can't attend. He can't even let class out *early*; he's paid by the hour and the minute."

"Done that, too – last week both days."

The supervisor had difficulty contacting Cody to inform him that he would not be paid for the previous week and that his contract would be canceled at the end of the year due to "gross misconduct" and "falsification of pay records." It was so difficult that she asked Evans to see him personally. At this point the police became involved. It was November 18 when a search was called. The mechanic was contacted, and when the lie was exposed, the most obvious possibility was that Cody had either gone somewhere unusual, desirous of privacy (pawn shops, open clinics, and banks were checked out and their employees questioned), or he had walked home. This possibility was shelved at first for being too illogical: why lie about a car's availability to your carpool in order to walk home? On November 22 a search was made of the three most likely routes to his downtown apartment.

……………

Deputy Sherriff Lee Davis Jackson led a detail of deputies and volunteers down the highway, scouring the ditches, then down Michigan Road. He calmly dissolved a spearmint lozenge in the pocket of his cheek, and swiveled his heel on the soggy carpet of rotten leaves feeling the course gravel beneath the pulp. The search party was extending down Hatcher Hill Road, knocking on doors and questioning locals. Outside of a tall Victorian house an old man played with a golden retriever while his wife and three grandchildren looked on. The porch and eaves were edged in faded gingerbread work and the blue slate roof was stained with copper-green streaks, and the man who owned it was brown and wrinkled and bent. Jackson approached the house while the detail wove between the guardrails and through the brambles. The old man caught his eye and shooed his family inside while he met the officer on his sidewalk.

"I haven't seen anyone like that around here, sir... Wednesday the sixth, you say?"

Jackson shifted the lozenge to the opposite side of his mouth and licked the fringe of his moustache.

"Yessir. We think he might have walked behind your house to get downtown. Might've tripped. On the maps it looks steep on some angles."

"You're not leading a rescue party then?"

"Body recovery, I'm afraid. That's off the record, though."

Some brush crackled nearby behind the leafless trees that stretched upward like iron bars. An even louder snap, then a garbled clatter of rocks against rocks followed by a series of gulping splashes. The two men paused mid-gesture. The old man's hands crawled into his cardigan pockets, and he began to look like a person who would dearly like to be in another place.

"Well it would be easy to fall off that trail. I only went there once when I was growing up. My two older brothers followed me down there and made me come back. After that my pa had those guardrails put up."

"You folks have had this place that long, eh?"

"Yessir. It was built in '87 – 1887 – by my great-grand-pap."

"He bought this land, then?"

"Well, more took it when no one else would. People kept off that trail back there. Some gone missing in my pap's time and in my grand-pap's. That's why they closed it off. The folks in the hills said it wasn't a right place, and when I was schooling there were all manner of stories of witch charms and floating skulls and men that walked like spiders But I never worried too much. Still... it just *ain't* a right place, you know?"

The radio buzzed. Jackson started, accidentally swallowing the lozenge. It was sucked down his throat and he coughed up a fleck of spearmint before he reached to his shoulder to engage the radio clipped to his epaulette.

"Just a sec. Yeah, go."

"Sir, we found a backpack and a coat. And, uh, there's smells, sir."

"I'm comin'. You folks you all have a nice day, y'hear."

The old man watched the younger man walk down the hillock and fling a leg over the rusted guardrail. Within three strides he had been swallowed by the fat trees and the shaggy brush. Overhead the sky had changed from jade to lilac, with grey piles of vapor collecting in the west and dampening the submerging the sun. He thought back to the day that his brothers had saved his life and nervously rubbed his thumb along his right forefinger where the flesh had been torn off and the bite marks still pursed his brown skin. Rapidly he turned back to the house, whispering a curse on the land and wondering how he managed to sleep so near to It.

When Jackson's detail managed to rig scaling equipment to the old overhang, they followed the trail, similar to those made by wolves and cougars dragging prey to their dens. They found Cody Lehman fat and black at the bottom of the ravine, in a burrow eaten out of the flint wall by melting snow. He was not alone. They were arranged in a quaint order, like dolls seated around a plastic teapot, generating a laughless, expressionless, lipless company. The forensic anthropologists brought in from Louisville closed the road off for three days while they unearthed, cataloged, and documented the collection.

OLD SHOCK
— David Senior

AS Paul approached the town the signal for his car radio began to fail. It seemed to sum everything up in a nutshell. Even national radio couldn't make it out to these coastal backwoods. Though the roads round this way were little more than single-carriage tracks most of the time, so why should he expect anything else?

Once again, he silently cursed his brother for coming out here.

He felt grouchy. It had been a long drive. However, even his mood improved at his first glimpse of the ocean – shimmering sunlight, reflecting the deep blue of the skies above – across the endless fields and towards the horizon.

He wondered whether city dwellers like him ever truly lost that childhood excitement that comes with seeing the ocean. Maybe that was ultimately the appeal of this place to Robert.

Paul drove past farms and woods and the odd campsite, towards the roofs and church towers beyond that marked the end of this leg of the journey. He kept fiddling with the radio but was getting no joy, only a blanket of snow and feedback over the music he wanted to listen to, so flicked it off.

He passed by the town sign on the edge of the village. It read, in big friendly letters, WELCOME TO CROWSMERE. Even driving, Paul could make out the graffiti that some wit had scribbled across the greeting: "This Is Where People Come To Die."

Paul smiled in agreement at that. At least somebody out here knew the score.

After all this, Robert had better be in. Paul had no intention of staying in this little inbred middle of nowhere village for long – he certainly intended to be sleeping in his own bed tonight – but the least his brother could do was buy him a pint in some local boozer for his trouble.

"Sabbatical." That was the word Robert had used to describe his year away from work. Not that it was hard graft to start with – droning on for a couple of hours a day in front of a few university students who would rather be out getting drunk and laid didn't sound exactly trying. The last time Paul had seen his brother, it had been almost a year ago at their mother's seventieth birthday dinner in the garden of a local restaurant. Robert had explained that he was taking the next year off from teaching to focus on working on his book. Their mother was, as ever, beaming with pride, and even their sister Kathy seemed to be at least feigning interest, so it was left to Paul to ask the questions like, "So, do you not get enough holiday as it is, then, with all the breaks the schools have?" and "So when are we going to see this book of yours in the shops, then?"

Robert had smiled coldly, and Paul, knocking back his umpteenth glass of wine – not his usual tipple, he must admit, and so was feeling a touch heady – felt a sense of triumph. Brothers they may be, but sometimes that speccy know-it-all needing putting down a peg or two. Later, he had overheard Robert telling Kathy that he was going away for a few months – spending six months renting some old dear's house in some poky little seaside place called Crowsmere, at the other side of the country – to aid with his research. "Research," Paul had scoffed, wandering back over. "I thought you just wrote about books other people had got round to writing."

"I'm writing a history of a folk tale specific to that region," Robert said, turning on him. He looked his brother up and down, disgusted. "I doubt you'd be interested, Paul."

"Oh, aye?" was all Paul could manage, taken aback by Robert's hostility, obvious even with his senses dulled with booze. "Just wondering, like..." he continued, before Robert and Kathy turned away and continued their conversation. Practically turned their backs on him! Paul tried to ignore the affront, but with everybody else at the table talking to somebody else, he earwigged his siblings whilst gazing out across the garden. Kathy asked Robert about the folktale he was researching.

"A story about Old Shock," he'd said. "The Devil Dog. Goes back hundreds of years. Haunts the cliffs overlooking the beach all along that coast. Lots of occult activity in that region, and a history of smuggling, so there are various possible interpretations of..."

Whatever, Paul thought now. A year off work to read about some fairytale nobody had ever heard of and the entire family fawns.

Into the village proper now, Paul examined the streets around him. A bonny enough village, he supposed, as he passed a row of flint cottages facing the sea, but he still dismissed the entire place as ultimately nothing more than a hole in which to dump pensioners on their last legs and spotty boy racer native youths who would probably spend their entire wretched lives here. He noticed a block of derelict-looking holiday apartments called Clifftop View Flats, and parked up outside there, unwilling to drive even longer looking for a car park.

He stepped out into the warm air, and stretched and rubbed the various aches in the small of his back. He looked around him. He locked the car and had a stroll down the promenade, past chip shops and amusement arcades and places selling souvenir tat. Nowhere was exactly busy, and even then it was mostly older folk wandering about. The summer holidays hadn't started yet, clearly.

He bought himself a bag of chips and ate them whilst looking around. He found a pub called The Trawlermen and took a pint out into the mostly empty beer garden. He sat in the sun and supped at his beer and thought about his mother.

The funeral was in two days. Kathy had found her dead on the living room carpet a week and a bit ago. The doctor told them it had been a massive heart attack. As well as arranging the funeral details – Paul was no good at that sort of thing, so just kept out of it – Kathy had tried constantly to contact Robert. Endless phone calls that were never answered, even a few letters. The problem was, nobody was sure if Robert was still away with his research or not. He certainly wasn't in his flat back home: Kathy had been round there several times, banging on the door, shouting through the letter box. Paul hadn't spoken to his brother since the meal and Kathy admitted she'd only been in contact with him when exchanging Christmas cards. By her reckoning, he should have finished up in this Crowsmere place maybe two months ago: all she could think of was he had decided to stay on down there longer, perhaps moving accommodation and not getting around to telling anybody.

Kathy had gone through their late mother's address book but couldn't find an updated address, only the one he had initially given them. The one she had written out for Paul after begging him to drive down to try and find him. Paul had grumbled, but relented.

Paul downed the remainder of his pint. He considered ordering a second, but already the beer and the afternoon sun were relaxing him perhaps too much. He went back into the cool darkness of the bar.

"Excuse me, mate," Paul said, calling over the barman, taking from his wallet the scrap of paper on which Kathy had written Robert's temporary address. "Do you know where I'd find this place..?"

It was only a few streets away, as it happened – though a village this size, everywhere was only a few streets away from anywhere else. Paul followed the directions the barman had given him. Number 17, Poppy Lane. The houses down this road were old, and high – many were guest houses or B&Bs. Paul figured the one Robert had stayed in would be the same, but, as he stood outside the door glancing up at the building, he noted only one doorbell, and it certainly looked like a single property.

Certainly looks like an old woman's place, too, Paul thought, walking up to the door. The tiny front yard was slabbed but covered in pots of flowers in bloom. All the windows had net curtains across them, but again, plants and knick-knacks (porcelain figurines of dogs and fishermen of such unironic kitsch that they turned his stomach) stood guard on the window sills.

By the house number on the wall by the door was a small sign, made from various pieces of sea shells and crockery glued together, with HAPPY HOME painted across it.

He pressed the doorbell.

A dog began to bark from inside, a deep, slow-sounding thing. Paul shifted on the doorstep and looked around him, watching an old silver-haired couple emerge from the guest house opposite and shuffle slowly in the direction of the beach front.

This is where people come to die.

Through the door, he could hear a female voice quietening the barking. A silhouette appeared against the frosted glass, and he heard a lock being slid back and a chain unfastened.

"Yes?" an old woman asked, peering out.

Paul had tried his hand selling double glazing door-to-door in his early twenties, and he lapsed back into that patter. He smiled. "Hello there, doll. Sorry to trouble you... I'm looking for a chap called Robert I was led to believe may be staying here?"

The old woman looked at him from beneath a bob of white hair, part expectant, part blank, as if to say, Go on.

"Er," Paul said. His heart sank as he began to worry if Robert had initially provided them with an incorrect address. If so, there would be hell to pay when he finally turned up.

"Robbie McIntosh?" he continued. "I thought he was meant to be renting this place out for a few months..." Still nothing. He wondered if the old dear was right in the head.

"I'm his brother," Paul added, uselessly.

At this, a light seemed to flick on somewhere behind her eyes. "Ah!" she cried happily, clapping her hands together. "Mr McIntosh, of course! I'm sorry, my memory isn't what it was... He is the writer, yes?"

Feeling irritation – how could he go round telling people he was a writer when he hadn't published a book yet? – Paul simply said, "Aye, that's the one. I'm afraid I've got some bad news for him."

{47}

"Oh dear," the old woman said, opening the door wider now. That enormous-sounding dog was still cough-barking somewhere out back. Paul nervously glanced over the woman's shoulder into the hallway behind her, but it seemed any angry hound was secured off in a room somewhere. "Mr McIntosh rented the house from me whilst I was away visiting my niece... She lives in Australia, such a nice girl, she's a doctor, they both are... Fifteen years they've lived there, you know, but neither one of them have lost a bit of their accents..."

Paul continued to smile even as he began to glaze over. "And my brother?" he managed to insert, gently but firmly.

"Of course," she said, as if that had left her mind completely. "I'm sorry, but he left here perhaps two months ago, when I returned."

Great. Paul sent another silent curse Robert's way. He looked up and down the street, pointlessly, as if he expected to see him happen to be strolling past.

"Do you know if he stayed in town?" Paul asked, turning back to the old woman's sympathetic eyes beneath her thick spectacles. "Did he rent somewhere else? Or did he leave you a forwarding address at all?"

"Please, come inside," she said, now moving aside and opening the door fully for him. "He may have left an address... I'll go and see."

Paul thanked her and stepped inside. She closed the door behind him. The hallway was dim, its only window that in the front door. The dog seemed to know a stranger was inside, and upped its enraged barks. The old woman ushered him through a doorway off the hall on the right. "Please, sit down, dear... I'll see if I can find anything. Would you like a cup of tea?"

"No, thank you," Paul said, stepping into the bright lounge. "I don't want to be any trouble." It was warm in here, bordering on stifling. He marvelled at how Robert could stay in such a place for six months. He'd always had an old head on his shoulders, but Christ, surely not this old. Doilies seemed to cover every surface, and on top of these were yet more revolting porcelain dolls and pots of pot pourri and vases of sickly-scented flowers. He didn't want to spend the afternoon stuck in here reminiscing. Although, as he thought this, he did feel a pang of unexpected sadness, and guilt. She was probably just lonely. Like his mother must have been at the end. Of her three children, Kathy was the only one to visit her with any regularity, and even then only once a week or so.

Paul had only lived a ten minute walk from her.

At the old woman's insistence, he perched politely on the edge of an armchair.

"All my paperwork is in the kitchen," she told him, about to leave the room. She was thin, and moved liked some eager if fragile bird. She turned back to him, and her voice turned a hushed tone of gossipy. "Is it... very bad news?"

Paul wanted to smile affectionately. His stopping by was probably the most drama she'd had since her holiday, poor old soul. He kept his expression respectfully sombre, however, when he said, "Our mother passed away."

She looked down at him like he was a five year old sadly cradling a popped balloon. "Aw," she said. "Such a shame." She turned and scurried away.

With her out of the room, Paul stood up, and strolled idly around the room. Framed reproductions of bland watercolours hung on the walls alongside black and white photographs of people he assumed to be long gone. Men and women posing on the beach in enormous swimming outfits, or smiling at the camera as they tramped heartily across rugged moorland. One particular couple appeared in the photographs more than most – a robust gentleman with a receding hairline and a slight, dark-haired beauty. He wondered if this was the old woman in

{48}

younger days, with a now-deceased husband. He peered at the pictures but couldn't really tell.

"Are you sure you wouldn't like a cup of tea?" she called out from another room.

"No, thank you," he shouted back, turning towards a glass cabinet in which there stood more smaller framed photographs. Paul didn't have a single photograph on display of any of his family or friends in his flat. Any that he did have were kept in no particular order in a shoebox in a drawer. He wondered whether this would change, the older he got.

That dog continued its weird barking from somewhere. Paul wondered whether Robert had had to look after it whilst the old woman was away. She surely couldn't have taken it to Australia with her. If it barked like that all the time, it would have been impressive for Robert to manage any work at all.

Paul picked up a small lucky cat figurine from the mantelpiece. He scoffed. It would have been ghastly enough even had it been finished correctly, Paul thought, but to make things worse it had then been mispainted slightly, so its face looked like it was sinking on one side, like the poor creature had suffered a stroke.

Homemade gift, he figured, placing the thing back.

He sat back on the armchair. He felt restless, wanting the old woman to return with an address so he could get out of this slightly sad, stuffy front room.

On a small coffee table beside the armchair was a pile of books and magazines. He uninterestedly looked through them as he waited. The top few were knitting and crochet magazines, then a notebook, then a fairly weighty and highbrow-looking tome bearing the title Eastern Counties Folk Miscellanea. He lifted it, intrigued – plain cover, cloth-bound, more the kind of thing he'd have expected to see in an antique shop or dusty college library. The kind of book he would have expected to see on his brother's shelves.

He turned the book over, and noticed several scraps of paper sticking out from a section near the middle. Paul opened the book to this section, where he found a chapter headed 'Old Shock and the Daemon Dogs of the East Coast.' He flicked through the pages. The pieces of paper, he was unsurprised to see, were covered in notes. Paul recognised his brother's handwriting.

Out in the hallway, he could hear the old woman finally coming back. She seemed to be chattering to herself. Paul stood up, still turning the pages of the miscellany, wondering whether she even knew Robert had even left the book when he had departed. He looked at reproductions of medieval woodcut images, of enormous snarling beasts and witches and the devil, and his eye fell upon a note Robert had jotted: "Shock – Shuck – old Eng. 'scucca' – 'demon'?"

"Did you know this had been left here..?" Paul asked, turning round, before the words died in his throat.

He paused, and was about to laugh, unsure how else to react to the sight – baffling, and clearly some bizarre joke. Yet as his naked brother lurched on his hands and knees into the room, the thick collar around his neck attached to the leash being held by the old woman behind him, Paul didn't even know how to laugh. Robert, never a bulky man, was now a lean, wiry creature, muscles tensing beneath skin intersected everywhere with scars and lash marks and thin scabbed wounds. Dirty hair hung long and a straggly beard covered his lower face.

"Robert," Paul said dumbly. Through some instinct, he took a step backward. The heavy book dropped from his hands, forgotten, onto the thick carpet.

Robert snarled, and barked – ludicrously, actually bearing his teeth, and here Paul actually did laugh, stopping only when he noticed Robert's hands. Robert was on his hands and knees, but did not have his palms flat against on the floor – rather, he had both hands curled backwards, wrenched and knotted, and was moving forward with that hideously off-kilter movement with his upper-body weight resting on his twisted bent wrists.

The old woman, standing behind Robert, the thick lead clutched in her fist, had her eyes closed, her head titled up, as she muttered what sounded to Paul like an endless stream of gibberish.

Paul began to crouch, slowly. Robert barked, saliva flicking from between his teeth. Paul's eyes flicked from those of his brother – raging and unrecognising and utterly alien – to the multitudes of sore wounds across Robert's body. He held out his hands in front of him, calmingly.

The old woman's chanting became louder, and more shrill.

"Robert...?" he managed.

Then the lead in the old woman's grip was freed and Robert lurched crazily forward and was upon him, knocking Paul back in a blur of snarling and hair and arms and unwashed stench and surprising weight. Paul fell back against the carpet, knocking over the coffee table and sending magazines flying, too bewildered to think about defending himself even as his brother's teeth bit down into his Adam's apple and wrenched away meat and splatter and cartilage. Paul could hear the old woman's babbling even as the crimson mist stung his eyes. Robert was back on him, biting down into his face.

Paul eventually tried to scream, before realising he was simply choking on and gargling out his own blood. His hand, pinned uselessly beneath him, gripped onto the carpet. The carpet felt thick, comfortable.

THE END HAS NO END
— Geoff Woodbridge

HE'D been lying awake for hours, just gazing through the white linen sheet which half covered his face. The sunlight, which crept through the gap in the blinds, washed over the room turning everything golden. It was a fresh crisp beautiful day outside. It was quiet. Liam lay; waiting, thinking and remembering the past few days. He could hear his heart beat, slowly; the slight whisper of breath, whistling through his nose. He'd mostly spent time on the playstation, destroying worlds, shooting aliens and racing fast super cars in an almost realistic virtual world. He'd watched movies and played music as loud as the speakers could take without distorting to the point of incoherence and deafening, whichever came first.

He pulled the sheet back and swung his legs out of bed, leaving his room in a state of chaos. He walked down the corridor in his underwear to his fathers study. His pale white skin raised goose bumps to the shaded morning air. Turning the crystal handle, he entered and approached his goal, the reason he had eventually left his bed. The 1958 Fender Stratocaster, his Father's guitar. A US edition, not like the modern Japanese remodels. Cream body with a black polished fingerboard and a maple neck. He picked it up and threw the strap over his head, whilst flipping the amp on in a single movement. There was a soft buzz of warm power. This was his fathers pride and joy. He'd bought it several years ago, not as an instrument that he could play, but as a reason to learn, after years of strict routine at sea with the navy, this was his chosen route to self-expression: He couldn't play a chord. He was a skilled engineer, precise and accurate. A thinking man with a fast mechanical mind, unfortunately, this came at a cost and a genetic deal for lack of creativity. Liam, his only son inherited his engineering brain, but also gained his creative heart from his mother. She was a gardener by trade, loved flowers, Orchids actually, breeding all sorts of exotic strains and rare super plants. She was an artist and poet. Liam remembered her soft voice reading poetry to her plants. She'd mentioned they required intellect as well as good water, sunlight and soil to develop as a truly beautiful flower. Liam hit a few chords, the sound filling the family home with echoing distortion. He stood with his legs wide apart, swinging his arm around and around, with each pass, creating a deafening thunder, eyes closed, playing to an audience of a million worshipping fans. His arm's spinning rotation, windmill sail, slowed to a stop raised high above his head: a rock and roll salute whilst the sound from the amp soothed to a quiet hum. He opened his eyes. From this room, he could see out across the field to a few of the neighbouring homes. He walked towards the large sash window, guitar still in place, covering his underwear. Any passer by could see there was a teenage kid, playing guitar naked at the window, but he knew there was no-one watching. He knew there was no-one really left. This was an idea, a conclusion based on two things. The previous few day's events and an interest in cheap, end of the world horror films.

Three days earlier, he'd spoke to his father. It was a brief phone call, neither really wanted, which was mainly one of necessity. They'd had words prior to the call regarding Liam's behaviour in the town, a situation wrongly reported and as always, the UK's legal system of innocent until proven guilty need not apply in Liam's case. The result was an unspoken agreement of civil communication.

'Liam, it's Dad'

'Hi"
'I'm with Helen. We're at the Hospital. They're keeping her in'
'OK.'
'Are you ok?'
'Yes.' Liam replied, softly.
'Listen, there is something going on. A lot of infected people here. Keep the windows closed and stay in doors. I'll call you later.'
'OK.'

Click, went the receiver. He hadn't called back, not yet. For the next few hours, Liam had checked his mobile phone for missed calls. It got late. He'd locked up, turned out the lights and tried to sleep. This was the first time he'd been home alone. He lay awake, watching the shadows. Lights across his ceiling as cars passed by. He thought of his fathers words. 'Infected people.' His mind spun a Sci-Fi story line, blood thirsty beasts running through the countryside of England, loved ones transformed through viral infection, a chemical leak or military experiment for advanced warfare gone wrong. He thought of Helen, his father's wife. She was only seven years older than he was. A younger model to replace his mother, she'd moved into their home literally weeks after his mother's death. He didn't blame her, or hate her. He just accepted that this was his father's choice although he had no plans to accept this girl as his new mother. He mostly kept out of her way when he could and ignored most of her requests to turn down the music. She'd been with them for a year or so. The scent of the house had changed over night, from a soft refreshing, calming one to something of thick chemical infectious mass production; as fake as the colour of her skin.

His fingers moved slowly up and down the strings, bouncing lightly, pinging soft light chimes of single notes which seemed to bounce and return around the room. The roads outside were empty now, as were the fields, lost of their white cloud figures. Beyond, a small forest, offered a boundary between Liam's world and the infected outside. He watched, imagining the diseased, staggering, approaching, craving flesh, his white flesh. He leant back, resting against the desk, watched the road awaiting his fathers car and the return of Helen.

The rest of the day passed without incident. It was quite outside, a beautiful bright day. From the kitchen window, Liam watched the pigeons flit from one branch to the next, in trees that swayed gently in the light summer breeze. He cooked some beans in a pan, opting to eat with the wooden spoon to save on the washing up. The wash-basin was already overflowing with bowls and plates clambering to escape their watery grave. He tried the phone again but got the same familiar beeping tone. The afternoon followed with more guitar, a movie and an hour or two racing virtual motor bikes through fantastical neon streets. Then the CD came to mind. He'd been a fan of the New York indie rock outfit, The Strokes for several years, had instantly fell for their sound after hearing them being played constantly over a span of a few days on the radio. Like fate and synchronicity, they had come into his life and he embraced them with his mind. He bought posters, magazines with interviews, CD's, t-shirts and all sorts of paraphernalia. It was his thing, his way to express the way he felt inside as if the music read his own emotion and projected it back for only Liam to hear. A reckless, romantic, jangling, distorted sound, harmony between vocal and guitar, the theme tune for his life. Their new long awaited CD had been released the previous week. He'd pestered

Helen for a lift into town to the local store, negotiating a joint trip when it was convenient for her.

He ran to the front door in the kitchen and peered out through the circular porthole styled window, which overlooked the courtyard of the house. There was Helen's car, a design classic from the 90's, built to withstand any apocalypse: Safe, solid and rusting at the seams. At least his father had taken Helen in his own car to the hospital. Liam remembered leaving his new CD in the side panel of the passenger door. His hand fell to the door handle with his father's words filling his mind. 'Keep the windows closed and stay in doors.' Beside him, hanging up next to the door on a selection of wooden pegs, were various sets of keys. Amongst them were Helen's set for her car; An oversized fob in the shape of a Japanese drawn white cat with a pink bow in its hair. Tempted, he thought he could be out of the house, across the courtyard and into the card and back in less than thirty seconds and didn't believe he could fall victim to the epidemic virus. Maybe he could hold his breath? He pressed the handle down slowly, hearing a click from within the internal locking mechanism. Liam inhaled slowly. A deep churning filled his gut as his chest heaved, feeling an acid crawling up through his throat, filling his mouth with a warm sour taste. He pulled the handle back upright. He was sweating, his heart racing. He sank to the floor, clutching the keys. Fumbling in his pocket for his mobile, he tried his father again, fingers fumbling on the keypad. Beep, beep, beep he heard as the phone fell to the floor. He lay next to it for some time, feeling the cold slate floor against his cheek, soothing and calming. Across the room he stared at a collection of framed photographs, holidays, family and his mother.

Four days earlier, during Liam's morning home economics lesson, an announcement was made by the headmaster. He was a short bald man with ambitions of acting on the stage – West End - whose dream was cut short due to lack of talent and an impossibly high voice for such a short, plump man. He stepped into the classroom and whispered something to the ear of Ms Schaaf, a teacher Liam was fond of whom he'd guessed was in her early thirties and single, surmised by the lack of rings on her fingers. She enjoyed floral print dresses and had an impressive grip when kneading dough. Liam watched her expression, which changed from a carefree smile to one of concern. She raised a delicately drawn eyebrow as the fat headmaster stepped forward and informed the class that school was to close early that day due to un-foreseen circumstances. Liam started to remove his white apron as he took a glace at his six muffins in the oven that had yet to rise and actually shown little ambition of doing so any time soon. The exit from the school was one of chaos, with children of all ages running and pushing, fighting, all eager to leave. A rumour of an epidemic spread though the corridors as quickly as the feet on parquet flooring. Some sneezing kids found themselves fall victim to the rumour, receiving slaps to the back of the head and even the occasional dead arm. 'Don't touch her, don't touch her, she's diseased,' was one child's cry as a girl scrambled on her knees to retrieve her text books from the floor whilst holding a large white tissue to her face, her red eyes glaring with hatred.

Liam lived a good fifteen minutes walk away from school but instead opted for the more scenic route, wandering slowly through the village. The streets had grown quiet after the initial rush of the tide of youths who had vanished into parent's vehicles or homes. Un-naturally quiet. There was a light breeze through trees, lifting leaves and branches that swayed and whispered. Along a narrow path, that ran behind some of the smaller houses in the village, Liam noticed a young girl in her garden. She stood deadly still, staring out into the woods. Her eyes were glazed, crimson and raw. Her skin was pale. She wore a white nightgown, covered in stains and dirt. Liam stepped closer to the fence that separated them, hiding slightly from her view. Her face was pale with elegant cheekbones, feline. She looked taller than Liam, thin, like a model in one of Helen's magazines. He couldn't take his eyes off her; she was enigmatic and beautiful in her distress. There was something about her, something animal, something dangerous. He watched as she swayed from side to side as if moving with the trees and branches, becoming one with nature. He listened to the sound, the whistling, whispering and watched as she touched herself, her fingers thick with what looked like dry blood as she moved her hands over her gown and squeezed her breasts, leaving filthy prints of her deed. Lifting her gown, exposing herself, her thin white legs were scratched and bloodied. Liam couldn't believe his eyes. He checked behind him to see if anyone else was walking the path and if this site had found other audiences.

He turned back to the garden. The girl was gone. He moved closer, noticing a break in the fence and pulled the plank to one side and looked through but was met with a very different face. An old woman screamed and swung a stick at Liam. He could feel his cheek crack from the blow as he tumbled backwards through the fence. She was shouting and screaming, as Liam struggled to his feet, slipping in the mud and undergrowth, he didn't wait for an explanation. He ran until the air in his lungs grew cold with a pain that filled his chest. When he stopped running, he walked slowly, checking behind him just in case the old woman had followed. He touched his swollen cheek which was stinging, wet with blood: throbbing. He looked at the blood on his fingers. He couldn't understand what had just happened, what he'd just witnessed but even with the ache in his chest and the pain in his cheek, he smiled.

He was home in time for lunch. He told Helen that the school was closed for the rest of the day and that he'd gotten into a fight on the way home. She didn't believe him and called the school secretary right away.

"You've been sent home from school for fighting!" she shouted, before the school message kicked in on the phone. This clarified Liam's alibi, which changed everything. "Do you want some soup?'

Later that afternoon, Helen pushed open the slightly ajar door into Liam's bedroom. It was a boy's room, with walls covered in pictures and posters of footballers and bands, cars and girls in suggestive poses. The wallpaper behind was totally obscured. He sat on the floor with his back against his bed facing a large TV screen as he controlled a virtual character - a semi clad athletic girl - shooting rotting zombies, heads splitting open as they attempted to claw their way into the real world through the screen.

'Why are all the characters in these games half naked?' Helen smirked.

'She's wearing shorts.'

'And little else. I wonder why you enjoy this?

Liam didn't offer a reply.

Helen looked slowly around the room, inspecting each picture and poster, raising an eyebrow like a tourist in a fine art gallery. 'I'm thinking of heading into town,' she said.

Liam dropped the game controller to the floor, spinning around to face her, 'really?' he said as a smile beamed across his face. 'Now?'

'Yes, get your shoes on.'

The character on the screen was left to be torn apart by the flesh eating beasts, groaning, chewing and breaking bones. Liam grabbed his dirty white All Star Converse and pulled them on, laces still untied, he picked his grey cardigan off the floor and his wallet from his bed and was downstairs before Helen had begun to collect her things from her room. He paced and looked around the kitchen, waiting. Then he noticed a figure approaching along the front path into the courtyard. A feeling of panic filled his belly. His face flushed as his wounded cheek began to throb. It was the old lady from the garden. He ducked below the circular window on the front door and slipped out into the utility room. The doorbell rang out.

'Liam? Can you get that?' Helen shouted.

'Jesus,' he thought. 'How did she know I lived here?' he stayed motionless, holding his breath, as if she might sense his living soul through the wall. The doorbell rang out again, this time with a frustrated urgency about it as the old lady held her finger to the button.

'Liam?' Helen called out as she came down the stairs into the kitchen. Approaching the front door, she caught a glance of him, frozen still, with a look of terror on his face, 'what's the matter with you?' she said, a question, which required no real verbal answer. She expected strange behaviour from her husband's son and was never really that surprised at his ridiculous actions. She opened the door to a torrent of abuse. A bitter, angry flurry of words flooded through the kitchen as the old woman pointed her bony finger at Liam, accusing him of trespassing and spying on her daughter in their garden, insinuations of being a perverted peeping tom.

Helen had a way with people. She could control situations well, calm, organise and manipulate the emotions of others. The old woman was soon under her spell, with promises of punishment and discipline and a written apology in Liam's own hand. They had discussed the incident that was swayed heavily against Liam's actions with very little explanation as to her daughter's peculiarity. Liam knew he would come out of his badly, as Helen smiled and apologised on his behalf, waving the old lady goodbye. He stood silent throughout the accusation and the whole ordeal and now awaited the wrath of his wicked stepmother.

'Just get in the car.' Helen said.

They travelled into town in silence. Helen weighed up the events in here head, carefully planning her next move and decisively stepping back from saying the wrong thing. Her style was always to offer the evidence to her husband as an impartial party, allowing judgement to be made exclusively by him alone - albeit, suggesting her own view, subtly - this way she walked the line of never being seen as an archetypical step mother. They reached town, parked up. Helen broke the silence. 'Twenty minutes, don't be late.'

It had turned dark outside, an early evening kind of dark with thick fearful clouds that threatened rain. The kitchen was lit by several dim lights from electrical devices, cooker, microwave and radio, all offering slightly different times in different shades of green neon. Liam lifted himself from the cold slate floor. He'd been dozing; dreaming things were back to normal. He could hear the wind pick up. A buzzing whistle, zithered around the kitchen from it's slight opening in the top window. A fault from when it was fitted, something his Father meant to get around to mending. They had moved to the house several years ago. The house was bought at a cheep price due to its location; a renowned lowland, prone to flooding. It was a steal. A Victorian detached farmhouse over three floors. They had invested heavily sealing the house creating a super home, making it water tight like a ship with secondary waterproof lining throughout the building's ground floor cavity wall. Silicon and steel using vacuum pressurised mechanics around the front door, or at least the front door that they used, was the original side door from kitchen to courtyard. This was replaced with a seven-inch oval external aircraft carrier door from a decommissioned ship. The real front door was now just for aesthetics, completely wax sealed shut. His Father had done most of the work himself and was proud of the finished result, safe and solid. The whistling window reminded him of this achievement. 'As long as it's not whistling below waist height, we're safe,' he would say.

  Liam tried to call him again but received the same beeping reply. He wandered around the empty house, listening to the creeks and moans from the house and from beyond as the wind encouraged the trees outside to sway erratically. He watched from the window, shadows deep in the forest, figures clambering through mud and mire. The wretched and diseased, crawling, clambering as the weather reflected their black hearts. Rain grew heavier as thunder growled in the distance, flickers of lightening offering a glimpse of those creatures hidden below. Twisted, broken and soulless. A new level of rain exploded, as the storm pushed out its second wave of attack, cracking at the window, collective tiny fingertips creating a singular repetitive hammering, threatening to break through. He could see his own reflection in the window, his own face tired and lost in the darkness. Outside, the puddles collected in the courtyard, potholes filling up fast as a tide began to flow across the land from out of nowhere. The forest was alive with movement, trees folding back on themselves as the wind lifted branches from the ground, uprooting Oak and Sycamore, strangling Willow and flogging Birch.

  Liam heard a crash from below. From the top landing, he could see down into the kitchen. On the slate floor, leaves and photographs floated on a sea of rain, his mother's face looking back up at him, waving goodbye, sailing away. He pounced down the stairs into the destruction, splashing into water to his knees, soaking and cold. Searching for the photograph, spinning and pushing items out of his way as his whole life floated through the home toward him. The sea became deeper to his waist. He waded towards the metal door, pulling at the handle, trying to lock the seal. That's when he saw the car move. From the circular window, Helen's blue machine slowly taking off, gliding out of view like a boat making its maiden voyage, a crew of ghosts. He reached for the kitchen window, catching the tail of the car as it disappeared into the darkness, it's destination unknown in uncharted waters. He turned his attention back to the photograph, searching for some time without success, before retreating to the safety of the upper floor. Wrapping his duvet around himself, praying for a miracle. He sat shivering, cold and alone. The sound of the storm was deafening. He pulled the duvet tight and listened to his Mother's soothing words in his mind.

 He awoke next morning. There was a still silence. Liam lay, still wrapped up tight and listening. He could hear his heart beating slowly and his own breathing, soft and gentle. Thinking of the girl, wondering 'Did she survive?' he thought of her eyes, red and distant, her pale skin, soft and delicate. He thought of the photograph, sinking under a tide of leaves, twisting and fading into the depths of the sea as Helen's car sailed past, transformed into an ocean liner, smoke bellowing from a funnel with music blurring out loud from its tannoy speakers. He walked to the window, his duvet around his shoulders like a King's robe. It was still overcast outside, dull and wet. As far as he could see, the landscape was torn apart. Trees uprooted, fields, once green now mud with the addition of a vast lake that sprawled. Objects floating and sailing along in the breeze. He sat by the window, watching, waiting. The lake slowly soaking into the land. The sun come and gone. Liam slept mostly, waking with the hope of improvement. He'd ventured to the kitchen several times for tinned food that he ate cold out of the can. The water had soon dispersed and the slate floor was once again visible under the chaos of flotsam and jetsam that was left behind.

   It was some time later when the sun began to shine bright and the water level soaked into the earth. He pressed the handle of the front door, and could hear the mechanics within, winding into action, unlocking its vacuum seal. Liam began to laugh. A torrent of emotion filled his heart. His bottom lip shook uncontrollably as tears washed over his face. He opened the door. The courtyard was in a state of carnage, despair and distress. He took a step, placing his foot out onto the dry earthen floor as he took a deep breath, he could feel a release, something natural, something fresh. He knew now, they had been cleansed.

THE BARRIER : NITS IN THE EYEBROW
– Don Swaim

THAT season, an unusually infertile period, my mother gave birth to only a few hundred of us, my younger brothers and sisters. Still, it was a warm and friendly time with considerable tranquility and gobs to eat. Ah, castanets and tambourines and cowbells and the revered Feast of Helminth. We'd gather in ever widening circles to sing the revered old songs and share the stories that had been in my family for generations. I remember Great-uncle Reprah dancing in that funny way of his on his three remaining legs. Grandma Esouheniw singing wildly off key to applause and cackling. And cousin Namgnuoy, a delightful idiot, doing stand-up comedy, impressions mostly, but true to the bone. "Take my wives... Please!" Nor could I forget Drawde, the political maverick in the family, forever denouncing our unpopular national leader as a moron—elevated, many claimed, by our politically-corrupt highest court. "A delusional imbecile!" Drawde would roar to gales of indignant laughter. He would get no argument within our liberal clan. As for my Uncle Nahte, quiet and often morose, he was off somewhere fighting the good fight as he saw it.

We are the Cheyletiella.

I'm middle-aged now, and tend to bore my favorite wife with endless stories of my youth and family. She's a beautiful female, her cephalothorax and abdomen tiny and delicate, her four pairs of short legs, like mine, culminating in narrow hooks enabling us to securely grip our Host without fear. (So as to not misunderstand, when I use the term Host I mean the sublunary sphere, terra firma, Our Very Earth—that which makes it possible for the Cheyletiella to exist.) My wife's eyes, pedipalps, and mouthparts stimulate me beyond reason, as evidenced by our many thousand offspring. How my tibial thumb and tarsal claw readily grasp her posterior leg, the ventral surface of her abdomen curving upward to allow ready entry of my dilator through the gonopods of the vaginal orifice, and how I absorb her many pungent odors. Over the past two years alone—by the Cheyletiellan calendar a fraction of a fraction—she bore for me no fewer than five thousand larval instars. Each day I proudly inspect the eggs my wife cements to the giant pillars, which some call follicles, that spring from our Host to give us shelter. I'm paternally-proud of my nymphal entities, and who wouldn't be? Watching them develop their compound eyes, ocelli, and cerci is a father's delight.

But life's frequently hard, and our Host is not always hospitable. We regularly encounter monsoons, hurricanes, cyclones, quakes, and droughts. Occasionally there are efforts by some gigantic, unseen, unknown enemy to defoliate our sanctuary. More than once, an instrument even sharper than the cusps of our claws rakes across the soil taking with it many of us, but not enough to eliminate the race. Sometimes, great clouds of astringent gases, spewing from an unascertained source, seethe through our villages and towns. It's climate change, the scientists claim, although the unlettered among us insist the notion of global warming is a hoax. Do we really know? Can we really trust in science? Still, we survive. Many of our tribe attribute our longevity to The Divine Authority, hereafter known as TDA. Once, I was a skeptic, but no more, and accept His divinity wholeheartedly, even though I sometimes wonder how TDA can be so cruel even to those who believe and love Him unconditionally.

I'm one of the few Cheyletiella blessed with a higher education. I once ran against reactionary forces for high regional office, the Senate, and won. I tried to swagger in the mold of Uncle Nahte and busted a dangerous spy ring and two murderous drug smuggling operations. I won the most prestigious award my people offer in literature, despite my series of popular detective novels that made me incredibly wealthy. Most important, I devised a delicious sexual technique, which I have shared with all at no cost, that forever enhances the sensual pleasures of our race.

However... Yes, there's a however. The purpose of this narrative isn't to prattle on about my many accomplishments, but to recount the most momentous episode in my life: about the time I became an adult; about my sister Eibbed, a victim of the Sarcoptes; and about Uncle Nahte, who swore to kill every Sarcoptean he could find, and by his definition Eibbed herself.

Here's how it went.

I was in my late adolescence, and life for me and the others was idyllic. We ate and sexed and reproduced in tranquility until the vicious attack by a renegade Sarcoptean band that utterly destroyed our blissful paradise. Our foe came from across the wide no-man's land, The Barrier, where few of us dared to travel. It'd been so long since the enemy of old had appeared we were lulled into thinking The Barrier would forever protect us from our adversaries.

When the Sarcoptes attacked my family (cunningly, the foe hid in the shadows until we were sated after the revelries associated with the Feast of Helminth) they spared not a soul. Our communications apparatus was primitive in that era, and our runners failed to return with help in time. My father and mother were the first to die, crushed between gaping jaws, flexible stylets, segmented tarsus. As I saw my siblings being slaughtered, I grabbed Eibbed, the sister closest to me, and we ran for our souls, finding shelter behind a triple frond. I ordered her to remain still, not even to breathe. The sound of the carnage was awful, and I buried my head into the ground as if that could protect us. Next to me, I felt my sister, a mere child, shudder in fear. Suddenly, I no longer sensed the presence of her tiny body.

"No, sis, stay down. *Down.*"

Instead, I saw her wander back, as if hypnotized, to the scene of the atrocity. I was certain she too would be butchered. Instead, after completing their bloody business and feasting on the corpses, the Sarcoptes retreated toward The Barrier, my sister their captive. Hours later, quiet restored save for the swooping of the avifauna, I tentatively emerged from my hiding place. All around me were remnants of the slain, avaricious ectoparasites already starting to swarm over the bodies. As far as I could tell, my sister and I had been the only survivors, although Eibbed was now a prisoner of the Sarcoptes.

The rescue party arrived far too late. One of the them was Uncle Nahte, a bold adventurer who eons ago after an argument with his father—my grandfather—abandoned the homestead to fight in some now obscure war, Cheyletiella against Cheyletiella. We knew the dread Sarcoptes were not unfamiliar to him. He despised them with a hatred uncontrollable and had sworn vengeance on them. His betrothed was murdered by a Sarcoptean renegade, we had learned. But Nahte refused to speak of it, so we knew little of the details, except to hear him mutter, over and over, Racs Ecaf, Racs Ecaf, Racs Ecaf. At the time, I had no idea of what he spoke, nor did I have the courage to ask him. He always spoke low and slow, and never too much.

When I saw Uncle Nahte observing the carnage I ran to him, weeping.

{59}

"Buck up, Nitram." He put a stylet around my thorax as his four eyelits, narrowed in hate, studied the butchery. "The varlets. Our tribe massacred. All of 'em but you."

"No, Uncle Nahte, there's still Eibbed," I told him through my tears. "When they left they took her with them."

He spat. "Then I'll get her back. For better or worse."

"But how?"

"By goin' after them."

"Across The Barrier?"

"There are some things a Cheyletiellan can't run away from, Nitram. If the Sarcoptes can cross The Barrier, which they done more than once—and I can tell you a little about that—then so can I. Them creatures need to be exterminated to the last one. The world's gotta be made safe from the likes of such. But Eibbed…" His voice dropped off.

"Yes, Uncle Nahte?"

"No doubt she's been violated."

"What does that mean?"

"Means she's one of 'em now. Listen, nephew, you know what I feel about the damned Sarcoptes. One of these days when you're older you'll catch my drift."

I would—when I was older. But not then.

He wasted no time in gathering a posse willing and brave enough to traverse The Barrier into the land of the Sarcoptes. Some of his gaggle had fought at his side in his war. But the augurs professed that the cockatoos and nuthatches forecast divine disapproval, while the elders warned that traversing The Barrier alone would be suicidal. But Uncle Nahte wouldn't listen, which is why he was who he was and unlike any other Cheyletiella I ever knew before or after.

"We ain't stayin' here just to wait for another attack. And there's a certain Sarcoptean I'm in mind to kill. Let's commence, boys."

He turned and headed toward The Barrier in that graceful, almost shuffling stride of his, a kind of swagger. I ran after him.

"I'm goin' too, Uncle Nahte."

"That'll be the day. You're still a young 'un."

"Eibbed's my sister. You got no right to stop me."

"Too dangerous. You're stayin' home."

"I got no home. The Sarcoptes destroyed it. There's nothin' keepin' me here, 'cept you." I bit his leg, hard, and didn't let go until he relented, kind of chuckling as he did. He easily could have lobbed me off or worse.

"Okay, pilgrim, but you gotta carry your weight just like the rest. You'll get no favors from me. You wanna be a man then you'll damned well act like one."

"Deal. And I'm sorry I bit you, Uncle Nahte."

"Hell, don't never apologize, Nitram. It's a sign of weakness. Besides, it didn't hurt none. Now saddle up, like they say, on account of we're burnin' daylight."

We left with ribbons flying, bugles blowing, drums tapping, and choruses of inspiration galvanizing us. It was glorious at first, our cause righteous, but our odyssey proved to be long, too long, too hard, too deadly. The journey from beginning to end took twelve years by the Cheyletiellan calendar. The Barrier, arid and empty, had none of the dense foliage in which we were accustomed to finding shelter and safety. And there was nary a road house, gin mill, speakeasy, or honky-tonk—not to mention a chop-suey hole, greasy spoon, drive-in, or grubby pizzeria. Each of us down to Uncle Nahte would have given his left elcitset to happen upon an ice cream parlor, beer garden, or even some pestiferous clip joint. It was not to be. There were no scenic overlooks or sanitary loos either. At first, we didn't lack sustenance. Blessed with retractable stylets, all we needed was to thrust them into the ground to produce nutriment. But the fleshly nourishment gradually receded into uneatable filament, and I was certain we were going to starve. Desperation and Uncle Nahte's strong-willed example inspired us to live on our fat and to push on.

One sleepless night, Nahte approached me as I sat hunched by the campfire, scribbling.

"What you writin' there, nephew? Ain't some namby-pamby poetry, I hope."

"My journal."

"What's it for?"

"Sos I can refer to it when it comes time to write my book about all this."

"That'll be the day. Anyway, if that ever happens, which I doubt, make sure you spell my damned name right."

One year out, we were attacked by an appalling flying species known as the Pulex. I'd read about them in biology class but had never encountered any. Fat and green with lethally serrated mandibles, they swooped down on us, pecking at our sensilla and flagellomere. We might have croaked, been eaten alive, had not a whirlwind developed. In the bedlam we managed to escape. Single-handedly, Uncle Nahte cut down one Pulex made dizzy by the vortex, and we lived on the remains for two months.

The next year, in the exhausting heat, we encountered what appeared to be an enormous black dome, at least three fronds high, greasy, pulsating.

"Fall back," yelled Uncle Nahte. "That thing detects anything with heat."

"What is it?"

"A damned Ixodoidea."

"Is it alive?"

Even before I could be embarrassed by my obtuseness, something appearing to be a mouth opened and spit forward a harpoon-like tongue that impaled two of our warriors. In mere seconds their bodies were within the Ixodiodea's colossal jaws and swallowed whole. As the beast digested its prey, the rest of us escaped, finding safety in an arroyo.

"Talk about your blood suckers," said Uncle Nahte. "Only they don't stop with blood, but munch on the prothorax, scutellum, cervix, cephalothroax, and anything else the bastards find tasty."

One of the Ixodiodea's victims had been especially good to me, Esom, a cloddish but kind frond-gatherer who often shared his victuals when I felt faint from hunger, and who once nursed me when I fell ill with the lumbar beriberi, masticating his own comestible before feeding it into my mouth. I almost burst into tears at our loss, but was afraid of Uncle Nahte's recriminations. I did not want to appear to be weak in his eyes.

Nahte said, "In our world, Nitram, life's short, and Esom lived a hell of a long time. Anyway, death's part of livin', and not always the worst of it."

The perils we encountered as we crossed The Barrier were myriad, but the most intolerable was walking in utter darkness for nine months. Why the world turned totally black we didn't know, but it was as though a huge ski-cap had been pulled down over our vertexes. Uncle Nahte's dorsal faintly illuminated itself for only ten minutes each day, and it took a night's sleep to recharge it, yet it was enough, barely, to guide us straight. To deviate from our direction might mean marching to where there be dragons and fiends and infernos and merciless death. Some wanted to quit, retreat. Audaciously, one of our party—a discombobulated tribesman apparently trying to impress his mates—challenged Nahte's leadership until my uncle slashed him with a spiracle and put him in his place. The malcontent was a debauched bark-cutter named Sral.

"I'll make you pay for this, Nahte." Sral rubbed his bloody tarsal as he growled between broken teeth.

They had once been comrades, so my uncle popped him again right good.

"You tangle with me again, Sral, and I'll deliver your damned hide to TDA personally."

Sral was degenerate reprobate, and I feared we hadn't heard the last of him.

Just before some of us, including me, were about to turn mad from the perpetual blackness, the heavens spread, dawn broke, and, rubbing our eyes, we found ourselves at the periphery of The Barrier into what proved to be a continental mirror image of our own bucolic land, although a territory controlled by a brutal, violent sodality that showed no mercy. Still, it was comforting in some way to confirm that we Cheyletiella weren't totally alone in the cosmos, that there were others like us for better or worse. This distant side of The Barrier, similar to ours yet strange, was deeply foliaged, but was eerie, and all of us felt the presence of unseen eyes.

"They's watchin' us," Uncle Nahte said.

"I feel a fright, Uncle Nahte. I hate to admit it, but I do."

"Hell, every fandango is fought by a scared Cheyletiellan who'd rather be somewhere else—anywhere else." He turned to Sral, nursing his hurt jaw. "Where'd you want to be right now, Sral?"

Still angry, Sral turned his back, snarling, "Fuck you, Nahte, I don't have to tell you nothin'." Then he pivoted. "But, hell, I'd cotton to be back in Little Anal Annie's Pub with a puss on one knee and a vixen on the other suckin' on a straw of lunatic soup. But that's none of your damned business."

"Hold your water, Sral."

"Didn't you just hear me say fuck you, Nahte?"

"I never heard that. And you better be damned glad I didn't."

Uncle Nahte sent Cap Notyalc ahead with two of the boys in a scouting party. When the three didn't return we gingerly nudged ahead. Two of our party we found dead, their cranial plates all but detached. Cap was still alive, although his entrails were dangling like a scuttle of acanthocephala.

"We got bushwhacked," Cap managed to utter, spitting blood, his labrum quivering, minutes before he bought whatever TDA had in mind for him. "Damned sad I am to have disappointed you, Nahte." His final whispered words were, "'Twas Racs Ecaf what did it."

"Like I figured," said Uncle Nahte. Then, eyes misting, he whispered into his late compadre's now deaf ear, "Hell, old man, you never disappointed me." He covered the dead face with a frond.

I asked tentatively, "Are you crying, Uncle Nahte? You?"

"Go take a leak, you little larva. You're short on ears and long on frass."

TDA be praised, maybe blood flowed through Nahte's ostium after all, but now wasn't the time to find out.

"Uncle Nahte, what's a Racs Ecaf?"

He snorted and turned to leave, but stopped short.

"Okay, sit your dumb dnih down and I'll tell you. No, never mind, don't squat on account of this won't take long. Racs Ecaf's not a what, but a who. A certain warrior chieftain of my unfortunate acquaintance. Sarcoptean scum, he is. And I'm gonna kill him. But if'in I say any more right now I'm like to kill anything in sight I'm so pent up. So I told you all you need to know to stay alive."

I may have been a kid, but I knew enough to seal shut my labrum.

We came to a big, bald ravine, looking as though some vast metallic blade had slashed through a unibrow. On the far side of the chasm was a towering wall pitted with protective crevices.

"They're there and we're here, so this is where we're damned gonna stand," Uncle Nahte said. "Let the savages come to us."

To reach us the enemy had to abandon their fort and cross a naked, unprotected tract that rendered them vulnerable, and when they foolishly attacked we astonished them with our ferocity. We threw all we had at them, using our stylets and pretarsal claws relentlessly. We showed no mercy. Their survivors, stunned by our fury, retreated in chaos far beyond their pitiful, worthless wall. I wanted to pursue them but Uncle Nahte held me back.

"We gotta tend to our wounded, and we need to rest. They ain't no match for us. We'll pick up the chase at dawn."

This time, we had the advantage while the despised Sarcoptes were in disarray. The next day, we stumbled onto a Sarcopte village. It was mostly abandoned, save for a few old men and women and some kids. We lined the villagers in a row.

Uncle Nahte said, "We're here to locate a young Cheyletiellan female. Name of Eibbed. Where is she?"

No response.

"Speak or die."

No response.

Uncle Nahte summarily executed a white-tufted grandfather where he stood, an example chosen because, dorsoventrally, he was near his expiration date.

"Who's next?"

A granny, wrinkled, fluttery, and frightened, allowed that Eibbed was one of the females belonging to Racs Ecaf, and that he'd retreated with his wives and warriors in order to regroup. But there'd been dissention, she admitted, and many of the Sarcoptes had rebelled against Racs Ecaf. In fact, their entire nation was in disarray. Uncle Nahte ordered the execution of the villagers, all except the granny. I begged Uncle Nahte not to be so harsh, but he shoved me aside.

"Pity ain't for me, nephew. Out here, due process is a spiracle in the gut. Now focus on our mission, your mission. We ain't here for our health."

"But the granny said the whole country's in chaos, that they're in rebellion. If we annihilate entire villages they're going to hate us after it's all over."

"Listen, boy, lemme tell you the only thing you need to know in life. When you got your adversaries by their scrotums their hearts and minds will follow. But you got to squeeze first, and that's what I'm doin'. We got a whole nation to conquer, not just a village."

After torching the hamlet, we pushed on. Along the trail we encountered panicky, fleeing Sarcoptes, too many too kill, so we let most of them live, but not without beating them with the savagery Uncle Nahte believed they deserved—except for one comely female Sarcopte, barely of age, that he, defying all reason, seemed to take a shine to, although he tried not to show it. In her innocence, she faithfully followed him like a half-pint ydoat, and he didn't rebuff her, and when one of our boys, as usual drunk on fermented fluid, attempted to molest her Uncle Nahte knocked him on his meaty skcottub. It was Sral, of course. Always Sral. Soused without fail.

Nahte shook his head in disgust, telling me, "Life's tough, but it's even tougher when you're stupid like Sral."

"Then why don't you personally deliver him to TDA like you said you would? Let our holy avatar have His way with him."

"And why don't you get off your ecdysis and suck up your damned evaporated milk?"

I didn't find out until the later crossing about how Nahte and Sral had served in the Great Rebellion together, their long ago war, which somehow united them in ways no one would understand but them. Even if I had known, I'm not sure it would have mattered at the time.

After two more days of relentless marching, we came to a darkling grassland bordered by steep bluffs, where we found the remnants of our enemy, no longer the arrogant warriors of before. We saw them scattering fearfully into the hillocks and gave pursuit. I tried to stay close to Nahte but he sprinted far ahead of me. Out of breath, I watched from a knoll as my uncle, in a rare lack of judgment, somehow allowed himself to become hemmed in by boulders on three sides while three treacherous Sarcopteans leapt from their hiding places in a furious attack.

I screamed, "Ambush!" I know Nahte heard me, but I was too far away to help.

Wounded, outnumbered, back against an escarpment, Nahte faced certain obliteration. Then I observed Sral standing stiffly mere yards away, watching, only watching.

"Damn you, Sral, do something," I hollered. If he heard me he paid no mind.

Uncle Nahte might have been Sral's enemy as much as the Sarcopte, and it appeared Sral was going to let him meet TDA well before the end of Nahte's personal millennium. Held fast and about to be impaled, Nahte was this far from death when Sral, apparently with a change of heart, exploded from behind the Sarcopteans, his stylets and pretarsal claws catching the enemy by surprise, making quick and brutal work of them.

I got there in time to hear Uncle Nahte say, "By TDA, you saved my damned ecdysis again, you dumb bastard."

"Hell, Nahte. You got us this far. Besides, back in our war after I rescued your molting exoskeleton you told me a guy's gotta do what he's gotta do."

"Looks like I owe you another one."

"Yeah, you do. Not the least of which is my teeth, some of which you knocked out."

"Which you richly deserved, you dumb scuzzbag. Still, I gotta ask, and it takes a lot of deez nutz on my part. What I mean to say… I mean, if you'll jot down one more checkmark on my IOU. My nephew here… He, he…"

"Spit it out, Nahte. What about him?"

"Sral, if it comes about that I ain't around no more, take care of him. He may be spindly, but he's smarter than he looks. Got book-learning, which the rest of us don't. Claims he gonna write all about this someday."

"Will he do?"

"He'll do."

"Ain't makin' no promises, Nahte. I'll think about it if'in I get some time to think."

We smoked out the remaining Sarcopteans from their lairs, dispatching without quarter all but the youngest and the oldest. But high on a bluff one burly Sarcopte, glaring down at us, stood tall and defiant, as if daring us to reach him.

Racs Ecaf.

Even from a distance, the jagged scar along his fronto-clypeal sulcus was pronounced. He climbed higher into the rocks, knowing the odds were against him, hoping to save his sorry ssa. But in vain. Uncle Nahte reached Racs Ecaf face to face on an outcropping, and in an epic one-on-one battle that consumed six days finally slit the Sarcopte's fused maxillae to the core and hurled the corpse to the immutable ground below. I shall not dwell further on the particulars of the celebrated deathmatch here. It has been exalted in song and story, and my own account of the contest won the coveted Reztilup Prize, remained on the bestseller list for a decade, and is now required reading in grades eight through nineteen. Not to mention the cinematic and theatrical musical versions, as well as an opera in three tongues.

Of one Sarcopte prisoner, a mere kid, I demanded to know the whereabouts of my sister. At first adamant, he acquiesced after a few blows to his dorsal setae and pointed to the rocks, not far from where my uncle killed Racs Ecaf. A cave, the kid said.

I found Eibbed in the chalky chamber. Shaking, terrified, she was hunched on the floor.

"Don't be afraid," I told her. "It's Nitram. Nitram? Your brother? Don't you remember me? Came here all the way from the other side of The Barrier. It's been years, sis, but you gotta remember. Before the Sarcoptes took you away from us and made you a…"

She mumbled something, but not of our language.

"Sis, you're a Cheyletiellan. You can't have forgotten You're no more a Sarcopte than I am. I know they tried to turn you into one, but…"

"Brother?" she said finally.

"Yes, yes."

"Mine?"

"Yours."

"Nitram?"

Suddenly, a huge silhouette loomed across the mouth of the cave.

"Stand aside, nephew," Uncle Nahte thundered.

"No, uncle, don't do it!"

Neither of us needed to elucidate in any scheme, configuration, or matrix the description of the crime he was about to commit. I now knew what he had planned to do all along.

"She's been corrupted by the Sarcoptes, boy. They took mine, I'll take theirs."

"Your, your…?"

"My bride."

"Eibbed's my sister, your niece. She has nothing to do with—"

He brushed me aside like a mere microorganism. I grabbed at his tarsus, but he pushed me back again. As he bore down on Eibbed to kill her, she looked at him wide-eyed, guileless, and said, "Uncle Nahte?"

"Say what?"

"Uncle Nahte?"

{65}

"Huh?"

She reached out to him with her delicate tibial thumb.

Suddenly it seemed as if all the blood of pestilential fire and fury had drained from his body. He fell backward, a look of shock upon his face. It was as though TDA had reached into Uncle Nahte's heart through Eibbed's webbed flesh. In mere seconds the decades of sin and hate and wrath and iniquity and guilt were washed away, and he was cleansed in the blood of the innocent bmal. Had TDA truly descended from Above to intercede on the side of righteousness and virtue? I do not know, although the most devout among the Cheyletiella would call it a miracle, and elevate Nahte to the status of a saint. He was no saint, but he was my uncle, so I was not, nor am I now, going to abuse the notion. It also fattens my bank account.

Our enemy defeated, Eibbed saved, the time came to leave the land of the Sarcoptes and re-cross The Barrier to our own realm.

"Pilgrim, you're on your own now," Uncle Nahte said to me with no warning.

"Me?" My mouth was agape I was so stunned. "I don't get it."

"I'm stayin' behind." He nodded toward the young Sarcoptean female we had captured. Ydoat we called her, but only in fun. "Besides, someone needs to help rebuild this sorry land."

Something had changed Uncle Nahte's heart. Love, even in a harsh domain like ours, tends to conquer those too weak to withstand it—even him.

"She's too young for you, Uncle Nahte," I said, half in jest. "Plus she's an accursed Sarcopte."

"Her? Accursed? What the hell does that mean? Watch your maxilla, nephew. I got a few more good centuries left, enough to kick your dnih to hell. Besides, I know what Ydoat is and I damned well like it. I'm lookin' forward to it—if you get my drift."

"I think your drift means love."

"You don't know from anal butter. You'll have to grow up before you can make any sense about love, you piece of doo doo-eating larva."

He was right. I knew nothing. And what the hell was anal butter?

I said, "Then let's take Ydoat with us when we go back. Then it'll be love in all the right places."

Nahte scratched his nads. "If I did that I'd be doin' what that bloody Racs Ecaf did to Eibbed. Tomorrow's gotta be somethin' we learned today, so that's why I'm stayin' here."

"But we can't pass over The Barrier without you."

"Hell, you got Sral here. He'll get you across. Right, Sral?"

Sral nodded. "Not only that, Nahte, but after what we been through I at last seen the light, so I'm stayin' off the sauce for good."

"Not too good, I hope. Ain't never trusted a species that didn't drink some."

"But I ain't no leader, Nahte. You made that clear when you took out nineteen of my teeth. This here larva's grown up a lot since we left home. Let him do it. You said yourself he'd do."

Uncle Nahte laced a stylet around my thorax and said, "Okay, you lead, Nitram, and the rest will follow. Do a bit of good when you get back home, but if you say anything bad about me in that damned book you plan to write I'm gonna cross The Barrier and snap your dilator into three pieces and feed 'em to the ectoparasites. Now saddle up and get the hell out of here."

I reluctantly took charge of the crossing—Sral recognized my hereditary status and his own limitations—and he became not merely my second in command, keeping the men in line, but a confidant and protector. As he had Nahte, he saved my life more than once during our return odyssey, which is a subject for a later installment. Eight more years it took to again transverse The Barrier, and by the time we arrived home I was fully an adult while little Eibbed was, thankfully, world-wearied but freshly aware and mentally composed.

After our homecoming, my name—and Uncle Nahte's—became celebrated among our people. The tribe sent me at its expense to Cheyletiella State University, where I earned my BA, BS, DD, PhD, JD, MBA, and LPN degrees. This led to a seat in the Senate, and ultimately a celebrated career as an author. Sral became our Armed Forces Chief of Staff, a post he held until his retirement and which, after his expiration date, led to full military burial honors. Eibbed never suffered the opprobrium she might, despite her Sarcoptean taint, and married an industrialist who became incalculably wealthy after developing a revolutionary device involving subatomic particles binding electrical, thermal, and magnetic properties that may one day allow us to communicate with one another, even across The Barrier to the Sarcoptes, as well as to the far ends of our Host.

It's clear to me now there's a power in the universe greater than ourselves. Most of the time TDA leaves us to our own pursuits, and those of our species are born, live, and die unaffected by His anger or mercy. I've often theorized that a world vaster than Our Very Earth exists out there, *way* out there, but until we develop flight like the savage Pulex there's no way to reach it. One day it might be discovered—and this will sound absurd because it's pure speculation—that we're nothing more than nits living in the eyebrows of some Obscene Entity, we Cheyletiella who risked death to cross a desolate land in the space between one eye socket to the other. What is an Obscene Entity? A dumb guy with an crummy apartment in Hoboken who rides the PATH to Manhattan for a low-wage job he despises? A guy who patrols beer-stained singles bars from time to time to get laid, inevitably with undesirable women even more desperate than himself? In reality, the world is so immense it's beyond our comprehension. I'm an author. I made all that stuff up about human eyebrows and the rest. Hoboken? Manhattan? They only exist in my fevered imagination. After all, I am a but Cheyletiellan. And a writer.

LOST AND FOUND
— M. Grant Kellermeyer

HOLDING it in his hand, he watched the light pool in the glass and run down the silver in brief, sparkling flecks. Someone from above called his name and he instinctively hid it his pocket, leaving the place where he had found it. He looked up into the fire tower. Some movement caught his eye – a white shape bobbing side to side then falling down. His aunt was waving her hand from the lookout post one hundred feet in the air. Beside her were five indistinct shapes – grey patches sitting neatly atop dark oblongs. His sister and their four female cousins watching from the shadows. He moved away to avoid the sun that glared in his face and casually returned his aunt's gesture. His hand returned to his pocket. It was still there.

   The object in the pocket, the pocket, and the twenty-six year old man who wore it all currently existed in a puzzle-piece of flat earth made up mostly of patchwork farmland bearded by black groves of poplar and walnut, and the puzzle-piece was called Wells County. Wells County is in northeast Indiana, near the border to Ohio, south of Fort Wayne and southwest of Toledo. It's only notable town is Bluffton, the seat, but on its western side it fosters a small but respectable state park which is also of note. Its name, Ouabache, is the French rendering of the Indian word for the Wabash River (which transfixes it on its way to the Mississippi) and although the spelling proves a stumbling block to some, it is quite simply pronounced WAH-*bash*. In spite of this very simple program, the locals – even more so perhaps than visitors – delight in the somewhat dignified if erroneous pronunciation *wuh*-BAH-*chee*. It is far more likely that they have tried to exotify an otherwise mundane title with a touch of Indian gravity, and the custom continues on to the deep annoyance of the underpaid and underwhelmed rangers.

   Amidst the sprawling, endless farmland – dotted with copses, and ribbed with sun-whitened highways, Ouabache State Park nests several manmade lakes, a collection of brooks, streams, creeks, and ponds, and a beautiful though not necessarily impressive stretch of Hoosier woodland networked by modest hiking trails and pocked with electrified campsites where lonely packs of campers nestle during the summer months while the raccoons grow obese and arthritic. and the beavers slip into the water along with the bullfrogs, box turtles, and green snakes. It has unassuming stocks of small fish and maintains a lightly populated swim park, but the two boasts that it is comfortable making lie in its bison park – a modern marvel during the 1970s when the all but extinct buffalo were first introduced – and its fire-tower, the delight of some children and adults and the terror of others.

   It was from the peak of this great feat that the visitor's family was now scanning the landscape: the lake gleaming brassily, like a strange, tarnished mirror, and the bushy green woodlands fading to blue and grey near the horizon. The tower consisted of a tapered scaffolding of red-brown steel that ended in a wooden platform roofed with the same dusky material. Achieving the height was done by carefully marching up a flight of grey, wooden stairs that cocked in an ascending series of right angles, and shuddered with every footfall, sending the severest vibrations to the top flights, the worst of which were created by enthusiastic interlopers on those at the bottom. Like its counterpart in Babel, it was easier to digest from the ground, and brought escalating punishments to those who insisted on continuing the ascent. But the view gained from the top rewarded its worshipers enough to steel them for the even more harrowing return to earth. It was vast and wide, and while it was simple, unadorned Indiana woodland, it provided something – itself simple and unadorned – to the restless nerves of the soul.

    The visitor knew this because he lived in the county to the east and had journeyed up the tower once or twice before. He was, however, not an ambitious man and not an adventurous spirit. He preferred the earth, where things maintained their appropriate perspective: the sky was above, the trees ahead, and only the dead soil was below. In the most literal and appropriate terms, he was a grounded person. Shrugging off his family's entreaties to join them, he pretended to no longer notice and sauntered beneath the black arms of a slumbering beech tree. Here, while their laughter and shouts could still be heard rumbling off of the lake's surface, he reached into his pocket and removed it jealously. This is what it was:

    A wristwatch, androgynous and slender, with a silver plated band, a clean, postmodern face (the only hours represented were the quarters, 12 being a black diamond, 3, 6, and 9 being black dots), with two rectangular arms, and three odometers measuring the month, day, and weekday. 9,8,Fr. it said. This was the one drawback of the piece, for it was 6, 29, Su. Furthermore, he knew that September 8 was a Monday that year. And yet the arms were correctly positioned to 3:43. 3:44. He held it to his ear. *Shck-shck-shck-shck-shck-shck...* The gears shuttled dutifully forward, propelling the arms through time. He turned the watch over and looked once more at the inscription, traced in a floral, Florentine italic which announced *"Wherever you are will be my home."* It was quaint and sentimental, unlike the visitor, who preferred the ground and the shade of old trees, never being one to play loosely with gravity. He admired gravity and preferred not to treat it presumptuously. But the italic legend caught his eye and wormed its way into his dormant imagination. "Who were you, I wonder?" He wondered, too, why he had so instinctively – without doubt, hesitation, or consideration – cast the wearer in the past tense. But of course, it was because they were no longer the wearer. Past tense. The joints between the silver links were black with dirt and tarnish, the band itself was nearly brown with age, and the glass face had been opaque and yellow before he had cleared it away with his thumb. It had hardly caught his notice except for the gleam of the back plate in the sun.

    He turned back to the lake and his eyes fell on the tree where he had noticed it, a less than middle aged maple with the stump of a branch jutting through its grey trunk like an accusative forefinger. The amputation appeared to be due to lightning, which had left an angry black scar racing down the trunk and burying itself in the earth. It was on this peg – a white shock of dead tissue some five feet off the ground – that he saw the watch while his family first mounted the steps to the fire tower.

    There was nothing at all attractive about it in that moment. It hardly resembled its true nature at all – more of a twist of dead grass than a discarded watch – and there was nothing about it to lure the eye of a man preoccupied with fellow hikers or the earthy smell of the lakeside path or the hum of the creation that teemed around him, bristling with life and death and evolutionary ambition. But the visitor was preoccupied with none of these things, and the soft, milky glint of the watch glass beckoned him through the limp shocks of grass that crowded protectively around the tree.

His hand is stretching forward and it passes along the bark – dry and deceased – where the electricity had scored the living vegetable flesh. It travels forward. Now his fingers have found it – they are crossing through the circle of the wristband – and they are clutching. They pull it to his face. What is this, eh? A watch. Something someone left? He is wondering who. He is thinking a swimmer, someone stripping to dive into the lake and they have forgotten the watch behind. They might have looked for it. But they haven't been able to retrieve it, and now he is holding it, stretching it, chipping away the caked-on dust with a thumbnail. And now it is in his pocket, and now he is walking away. Funny, he thinks, that he should suppose it belonged to a swimmer. The lake is off limits to swimmers, besides which, it is revolting – lathered in black scum and green slime – a habitation suitable for fat frogs and weaving snakes and ghostly catfish. Not for anything human. Nothing human. He is closing his hand around it inside his pocket. He is hearing his name. But what a voice!

When his aunt caught sight of him, he was stooped over the lake with his hands in his pockets. Something stirred in the black water very much like a large fish. She remarked to one of the girls that it was a pity their father hadn't been able to come. He enjoyed fishing far more than any of them, and if the fish were really quite so large, quite so friendly, and quite so stupid, then he would have had a rare day plucking them out of the water. But she hardly thought he would have carted them of and dressed them for their dinners. There was something vaguely unclean about the thing she had witnessed breeching from the scum. Unwholesome. Hardly something she would care to eat, let alone take home with her. To take home such a thing! But it was no matter; the fish was safely in the lake, and her nephew was standing up and gazing out into its silver heart, where the scum receded, and the bald water ran deep and black.

They ran down to him – he wouldn't heed their calls – and finally she laid a hand on his shoulder. It seemed cold. But he turned.

The cousins flowed down the hillock like a parade of Russian nesting dolls: the Amazonian prima donna – a girl old enough to claim a monopoly on the comparative science of cosmetics, pop music, and boys, but too young to be allowed out of the house in her makeup without a maternal inspection and an inevitable scrub-down – led the other three who dutifully trailed after their elegant idol in order of age and thus height. The aunt and sister looked back to ensure that they made it down the slope without incident (the Amazon had demanded to wear wedges – rocketing her already precocious height – and there had already been three accidents). They streamed down – the younger girls desperately fighting to keep pace with the Amazon – and eventually circled around a picnic table where they broke ranks and swirled over the sandy earth and under the grey trunks of elms like pieces of paper eddying in a brisk wind.

Jabbering and yelping, they flocked around a brace of iPhones, absorbing themselves into the little tools and relishing their collection of portraits and landscapes. All the while he quietly ignored them and wondered what the humidity was. All around him, the chatter of life blurred into an abstract work of tones and vague harmonies: the frogs purring in the grass, the cicadas buzzing in the leaves, the mourning dove moaning an elegy in the old sycamore while a bobwhite, a whippoorwill, and a titmouse all prattled cheerily in a robust maple opposite. Crickets crackled under the picnic table, squirrels barked as they jousted up and down the sycamore's wrinkled side, and two small foxes slunk quietly in the yellow weeds that bordered the woodland, watchfully reconnoitering on the chipmunks and hares that would spring frantically from one meadow to another, from time to time. Amidst all of these symphonics – a winding blur of dissonance and harmony that wove from pitch to pitch – was the sound of human beings, hardly distinguishable from the titmouse and the frog and the cicada. Neither exalted nor diminished, the voices rose and fell around a larger tapestry of life.

 Outside of its sphere, the visitor became absorbed in his own iPhone, researching the origins of his new watch. It was a strangely anonymous piece of machinery, having no observable trail on the internet. Only the inscription, with its saccharine, unoriginal sentiment, seemed to connect the bauble to real life. Frustrated by his inability to scrounge up more information on his new possession, the visitor quietly returned the phone to his pocket – opposite of that which housed the watch – and sauntered off while his family clucked warmly to one another. The lake drew him to its side once more, and he stared quizzically into its murk. Nothing. It yielded nothing. Well of course it didn't – it's not as though a lake were a computer or a microfilm viewer. And yet he felt deeply compelled to search it, as if it was unquestionably connected to his little discovery. He somehow felt that with it he had acquired an inheritance – an inheritance the details to which would prove tremendously important to him in the future. He felt urged to unearth its origins, as though by taking it he had signed a very serious contract without being fully aware of its contents. It was a strange thought, and he laughed at himself, but it was a sense that was proving difficult to dislodge.

 The sun continued to beat down on the human beings by the lake, even as it settled down the sky, deepening from searing white to boiling gold. But the day was undoubtedly waning, and none of the human beings had planned to sleep in the forest, so they started to gather their trash and pocket their trinkets. After some lazy milling around the rubbish bins, they formed a column (the Amazon leading the company of cousins, her nine-year-old lieutenant struggling to seem dignified and pert as she attempted to match pace, and the other two hopelessly tumbling after them) and filed down the gravel path to the parking lot. The aunt (walking ahead of the visitor and his female relatives) was talking to her husband on the phone, while she dodged the horn-like roots and glinting webs that encroached ambitiously into their tidy path.

 "We'll be home soon, just heading out to the parking lot. Yeah. Yeah, oh, no, he had fun, too. Yeah, we'll have to tell Janice about it. I think she and Curt – no, no I think so. Oh, I don't know why you would think that. Of course! It could – well, yeah, sure. No, not really. I guess – yeah. Yeah, I'd say it was. Sure, sure."

 She nimbly stepped over a branch that had plunged into the little path, holding the phone aloft, and brushed away a fresh strand of spider thread, before returning to the conversation.

 "Well, all in all, it was a lovely day. We had all had a great time. I think we should come here without the kids. It's such a chilling little place… What? I did? I did not. I did. Ha! Well you know I meant to say cheerful. Ha! What a thing to say!"

 At the end of the throng was her nephew. Men over twenty-five rarely enjoy being carted with their cousins on play dates, and he was eager to get back to his home, far from their voices and empty thoughts, where he could make some coffee, turn on the air conditioning, lock the doors, and read a book. All by himself.

{71}

They piled into the van. With the sun in her face, his aunt looked from under an upheld palm and counted dutifully.

"Okay, let's be sure we have everyone. One, two, three, four, five, six, seven… Seven… Seven? One, two, three, four, five, six… Seven. Why… *Uhn, tuh, thr', f'r, fi', si', sev'*… Everyone!" she shouted, "stand *still!*" Her face grew grey and her eyes swam as if drunk, or suddenly having realized a horrible reality. Something passed from her face and it regained its resolve and its color. "Let's make sure we have everyone here. *Uhn, tuh, thr', f'r, fi', si'*… Six. Okay. Okay, good deal, people. Six it is. Everyone's in, so let's head out."

The aunt climbed into the driver's seat, but she was no longer smiling. She had unquestionably counted seven twice. The sun had been playing with her eyes, but it was an odd thing to know that you are right when you are obviously wrong. But it was only a small thing, and it was unlikely to affect anyone other than her, she told herself.

He was happy to be the first dropped off. Something on someone's shoe was dreadfully rancid – a wad of soft dog shit or perhaps the putrefied stew of a mushy chipmunk's corpse – and he was pleased to distance himself from his demonstrative, effervescent family members. His mother's suggestion that he emerge from his well-guarded solitude and enjoy a family outing in the sun and fresh air had been unnervingly misguided. The entire experience had soured him on the entire concept of family events for probably a good month or two. Until more of his cousins entered their twenties and developed a sense of propriety and personal space, he doubted Thanksgiving or Christmas gatherings would be anything but ghastly misadventures.

He walked onto his porch like a withered knight crossing his moat after a disappointing crusade, and pulled out the small collection of brass keys which would return him to the peace of solitude. The sky was still a wide swath of gleaming pink intersected by thin bands of electric yellow, but the far east was dark like spilled black wine spreading slowly across a colorful cloth. He flipped through the keys. Car. Work. File cabinet. Parents' home. House. He ran the blade home, to the hilt, and twisted it like a dagger in the intestines of a meddlesome enemy. The door gave and he stepped inside. The twilight atmosphere was compounded in his dark and breathless house, and he reached for a switch. His fingers struggled to find the familiar plastic board, and the nocturnal air pressed impatiently against his neck and shoulders. He thought he heard someone in the street call out to him.

He turned to look, but the street was under the purple murk of a century-old beech, and the streetlight was apparently either out or slow in turning on. He put his keys in his pocket and felt his new watch as he did. Still with him. There was the question again, soft and coy – almost coquettish – was it "can I come over" or "do you mind if I come, too"? Or was it "aren't you going to invite me in"? He wasn't sure – either about the words or about how he could have so many impressions of one muffled call. He stared back out to the street where the beech's shadow fell in jagged, dark wedges. Scanning the empty pavement he smiled dully at his mistake.

"Entrez-vous!" he scoffed, offering a welcoming hand into the threshold as he glibly bowed. He closed the door behind him with a scratchy laugh and found the switch. The bulbs ignited, jetting tremulous white light over the floors and walls, and he rapidly sloughed out of his clothes on his way to the bathroom. Before he pulled himself from his trouser legs, he extracted the watch. He held it to the light.

"Wherever you are will be my home," he read aloud. It gleamed energetically in the electricity, like a buzz saw eagerly awaiting the touch which will awaken its innate purpose to chew and cleave. By the time he had turned the bathwater on, converted it to shower, and crumpled the pile of dusty garments into a welcoming hamper, the sky was inky blue, with just a blaze of alarm-red skirting the horizon, punctuated at gaps by the black cones of pine trees, which stood out like vicious teeth in a red mouth. He stepped into the shower as the steam rose to the ceiling and smothered the mirror with white murk.

The visitor's aunt and sister were in the former's living room while the younger girls giggled sporadically in the basement, their shrieks slipping through the joists and floorboards like the smell of pies cooling on a kitchen counter, colonizing one room after another with fluid ease. His sister handed the aunt a ceramic mug in the shape of a grinning pumpkin. The contents were warm, whatever they were, since cinnamon-scented steam puffed from its crown like smoke from a cottage whose locked door and bright windows ward off the fears of a winter-ravaged night. The sister returned with her own mug and they turned the TV on to watch a movie from a previous decade while the girls downstairs roared and laughed. The sister was thinking about her husband who was coming home the next day from a short business trip to the coast. The aunt was thinking about her family around her. Neither of them thought about the visitor, who had been invited to watch the movie with them. His refusal, the aunt had thought at the time, was unmistakably resentful, and his attitude when exiting the van was like that of a delinquent freed from a lengthy conversation with a scolding teacher. After mulling it over for some time she came to a conclusion: she would not invite the visitor to family events in the future. He didn't enjoy them – in fact he made them worse by his very presence. If he wanted to come to any of them he would be more than welcome. He could always drive separately. But he wouldn't, she reasoned. And she was right, of course. But as she siphoned the mug's contents and curled into the couch's crook she wasn't thinking of her nephew. No one in the house was. The black and white flicker from the television fluttered on the glass in the windows and picture frames like an insistent blizzard. The porch light glazed the siding in protective orange. The door was locked. The house sat safely on its corner and thought of nothing beyond its secure walls.

When the visitor returned from the shower he changed into shorts and socks, reclining on his red-striped love seat with his feet perched on one arm rest and his head cushioned against the other. He closed his eyes and absorbed the lonely silence. He had turned off every light in the house except for the tall lamp in the room he currently occupied. It had four lights at intervals along its trunk, and was muffled in opaque white paper, giving off a dull, grey glow that could possibly be used for reading, but only with eyes pinched and book close. The lamp was positioned to the right of the doorway which led from the sitting room into the kitchen and thence to the rest of the house. Sitting as he was on the love seat, his back was to the doorway and to the light, and his face was to the opposite wall – some six inches from his feet. To his left was a coffee table, and on the coffee table were strewn a variety of utensils, books, papers, and gadgets. He reached to its cluttered surface to retrieve a book – *Into the Wild* – when something half-smothered and half-breathing caught his ear. What was it? A raspy, muffled chatter... He looked at the floor, aglow with scummy light. He set the book down.

Something stiffened in his back and he felt his wrists clench for reasons he couldn't explain. But what was this? The watch. He pulled back a leaf of newspaper and there it was: *Shck-shck-shck-shck-shck-shck...* He smiled and plucked it up and let it dangle on his finger. Then he frowned. He had left it on the kitchen counter hadn't he? This paper was a week old and he hadn't moved it since last Sunday, hadn't he? But he had misplaced sillier things in his lifetime, and he twisted his mouth as if to say "oh well!" and laid the jewelry on his thigh where it caught the gloomy light, watching him. He wondered what it was about the piece that pleased him so thoroughly. It wasn't anything he would ever wear: while it was androgynous it certainly leaned towards a feminine taste. He didn't even wear watches or even own one. But it was as though a piece of his soul or spirit or brain was reflected in it – some common impulse, or shared trait. The impression he found most tangible was the idea that it was like meeting a kindred spirit and inviting them over to watch movies together in silence. He laughed at the strange idea and turned back to his book about another man in his twenties who valued independence and solitude. He hoped the story would end well — for them both.

   He edged himself deeper into the love seat, edging himself into the crevice of the cushions like a man stealing into a cave to escape a rain burst. What a comfortable spot he had! He crossed his ankles on the arm rest opposite the blank wall and crooked his elbows beneath his ribs, pulling the book into his face as if he could disappear into it and leave the world of pain and reality. The windows were fastened, the door locked, the house dark, and the air conditioning purring thoughtlessly while it manufactured the 64 degree atmosphere. It was an escape, a sanctum. He regretted ever leaving his cozy solitude and damned his family for ever trying to excavate him. He pulled in lungs of air with the satisfaction of a lion in his den.

   But what a stench! He coughed out the sour air and wrenched his face. Good God! The trash had gone bad, of course. Another fact of life he loathed. Something he had pitched was surely fermenting in the ooze that puddled at the bottom of the black plastic shroud. It was a curdled, fishy mash, and the odor – though slight – was powerful. It wasn't as though the trash were in the sitting room (indeed, it was in the adjacent kitchen), but the small traces of stench that floated in to him were intense and stupefying. At that moment he began to wonder if he should take it out – the pungent flavor was like that of soiled diapers and bloated fish – at that very moment. But he decided to carry on with his chapter and conclude it before he lugged the bag out of his sanctuary and cast it out into everlasting night.

   A car pulled up to the aunt's house. Two men exited the vehicle, and their laughter clattered off of the houses and pavement as they mounted the porch. One rang the bell and they spoke in unmuffled tones while they waited. The door opened and an observer standing under the trees on the opposite block would have seen the two men being wrapped up in arms pulling them inside. The observer would then hear the voices grow distant and hushed as the little group slipped rushed across the threshold and the wooden and screen doors were closed and bolted. The porch light was extinguished. Only the streetlamp's green-yellow light intruded onto the lawn and eaves, and only a thin splinter of orange light seeped between the living room curtains to suggest the warmth and calm in that place. In all other respects it was a castle – a den for hibernation during the winter that swallowed all green and life outside its remote boundaries. Within the hour the sliver of orange had gone black, and by one in the morning the house was doused in warm sleep. The moon and stars were tucked in beneath colorless clouds, and unconsciousness seemed to pass over the town and the world and the cosmos.

The visitor had fallen asleep some time near midnight, but the building stench of the garbage had shaken him back to wakefulness. He was glad, too. His dreams had been wild and abstract – of evasion and discovery, of pursuit and capture – and the tangible sight of his apartment went far in relieving him of the anxiety. But the casual step on the kitchen tile restored all of his misery, and set an electric surge through his nerves and veins. It was a wet, floppy tread, like that of a person who steps naked out of a shower when they think that they are alone in a house. Four quick, unmuffled flaps assured him that it hadn't been an isolated incident. There again. But there was something else in it. Something heavy and leathery, like his visitor was dragging a drenched beach towel – more than a beach towel – behind it. There it was again. The steps were awkwardly paced, as if they were feet at all, but what?

The lamp was still the only light in the apartment, and its anemic, milky glow was blocked from intruding into the kitchen, which was a solid rectangle of unbroken black, but it hardly would have mattered: the host was incapable of turning his head. He wanted to! If he could only rally his courage and lean his head even a few degrees to the left so that he could peek in the direction of those fumbling, infantile movements he would, but he couldn't. He kept his eyes riveted to the beige wall, while his head sat frozen, some eight or ten feet away from the kitchen doorway, fixed and immobile like a moth paralyzed by a spider's venom and is left strung to her web while she waits for her appetite to build before draining him in her hunger. There was a violent tumble, as of a drunk person attempting to stand from a floor where they had been crawling. He felt his stomach blushing with terror at his vulnerability; it warmed and chilled in pulsations as blood gushed to his organs amid his brain's directive commands: fight or fly, defend or defect. But his heart was cowardly, and he refused to look at it. It might look back at him. But what? *What?* Why did part of him seem to understand what was happening while the other – the majority – was just as eager to believe it to be a raccoon who had broken through a window screen in pursuit of the rancid trash? And couldn't it be? But raccoons do not have mushy, squeaky flesh that rubs against linoleum like damp rubber, and garbage does not smell like that. No. Not even rotten bacon, which he had smelled once, or spoiled milk, or putrid fish rotting on a riverbank, both of which he had encountered on multiple occasions. The mockingly sweet, fetid stench – like the mash of vomited fruit punch and meat – was distinct from the wholly bitter or sour stench of rotten food. Sweet. Sugary. Syrupy. But how valiantly he had to brace himself to prevent the gases from purging his stomach! It seeped in stronger now, and there was another fleshy flop, and another. Hands. They were hands. His visitor was crawling on their stomach. But there: a long, awkward squeak – another – and now a series of scuffling slips and stumbles, but moving forward. Was it on its knees and crawling now? He suddenly realized that it was directly behind him. Look. Look! *Look!* He urged himself to face it, to resist it. But he couldn't, even as he shivered and bristled with gooseflesh, even as his fingers grew numb and trembled, his neck was locked in place, and no will power could inspire him to so much as move his eyes from the point on the wall where they were fixed.

It was only now that he felt a cold grip on his wrist. The watch was strapped tightly to him, and it clattered excitedly away, like a dog who scrambles at the first sound of its master's car approaching down a side street. *Shck-shck-shck-shck-*

shck-shck!! Then a plop. Muffled and dry. A hand falling heavily across the kitchen threshold onto the Berber carpet. The sitting room was swamped with a gassy stench, and for the first time he heard the visitor's phlegmy chortle as it gained him. He pleaded with himself, with God, with It, but he could not face that which crawled so industriously toward him. Something that might be a knee scratched slowly across the carpet, then the sound repeated itself, and the choked noises it made – a muttering, squawking, chatter composed of garbled words, but seeming to exude a sense of self-congratulation, encouragement, and giddy anticipation – were undeniably poised directly behind his head. *"Home, home, back home. Thug. Brute. Won't get rid of me. Nope, nope! Staying. Back home, home, home…"* He wanted to reach for the watch, to rip it from his arm, to turn against the crawling, mushy thing lurking behind him, and to hurl the clucking device at it before pushing it down and running for the door, but he didn't and he couldn't. Two sounds – like those of a cat who digs its claws into upholstery before clamoring up a piece of furniture – announced that it had grabbed onto the loveseat arm rest. And yes, there was the shadow. The beige wall suddenly went dark. But what thing was this!? The shadow was not a perfect silhouette, but the outline was not that of a human person. Not a living human person. And then the shadow began to descend, and he felt the first drop of water hit his forehead as it hung over him. The host felt his visitor's long, mud-encrusted hair brush across his left cheek, and before he could retreat into the black avoidance of his closing eyes, he saw the hand – mottled blue and purple flesh, drawn tight into the bones that broke through it at the knuckles, where the skin was slushy, black, and unbleeding.

The lake at Oubache State Park is commonly agreed upon by locals and visitors to be beautiful. Punctured by dark islets populated with shaggy patches of underbrush and tightly-formed poplars and elms, it sparkles in its broadest spaces and glowers underneath the bushy trees that form along its shallows. The islets are used by canoers for picnics, and some of the larger ones – still hardly large enough to be called islands – are provided with wooden picnic tables. The wood is grey and rotting, and the bolts are rusted orange, but couples are occasionally still spotted hauling baskets out of canoes, paddle-boats, or skiffs, and unpacking sandwiches and glass Coke bottles from their provisions. The lake has a history of attracting couples. Some are platonic friends – retirees, fathers and sons – who come for the feeble fishing. Some are young people who have just begun dating. Others have been married for some time. But it is common in any case to see a pair sauntering along the banks, crossing it in a skiff, or perching on one of its stalwart islets. Sometimes, on misty days, rangers have seen less appealing strollers, lone figures that hobble and totter. In the half-perverse, half-serious way that rangers seem to adopt when approaching local folklore, they have told me that the lake has had a checkered history with the lovers who frequent it during the months between June and October.

They did not tell me of drownings or murders or bodies that floated to the surface after a thaw, or of jealous wives or bitter husbands, of strained separations or threatened divorces, nor of early morning rendezvous at the lake – a spot with fond memories of an optimistic courtship – nor of men leaving the park with dark, nervous faces. They did not tell me of investigations into disappearances near the park, searches that only included the lake when stench began to bubble from the dark waters between the shore and one of the scraggly islets. They did not tell me of women desperate to maintain their abusive relationships, of presents given, or of presents abandoned near the site of a revolting crime. They said nothing of bitter spirits said to wander shorelines, or parts of the lake and shore which sensitive people tend to avoid, or areas where some become nauseous until they flee to higher ground and refuse to return, or anything at all about coaxing voices floating through the tarry water like a call being made from behind the curtain of a steamy shower, or of hands being offered in gestures of frustrated desire, or of the heads or shoulders – ghastly to imagine – which might be presumed to follow. They said nothing about any of these things, and why should they? There are newspapers and microfilm and search engines for that. The rangers said nothing about the man who was found curled on his couch four days after his heart had exploded, or the watch which the police found and collected – a responding detective recognizing it as being a piece of evidence in a cold case which had gone missing from the archives – or the way that the throat was passionately wrung and the head viciously knocked in post-mortem, or the agonizing stench that lingered throughout the house – a stench far worse than that to be expected from a four-day old cadaver in a house chilled by air conditioning. Instead, the rangers said that the lake has a checkered past, that it is not wise to visit it at dusk or dawn without someone else with you, and that yes, there are lots of rumors about some of the events that have been connected with it. The ranger looked at me pleadingly after I had tried to extract a more full account, and with that I closed my investigation. I turned my car around and left the park, and he returned to his hut. Although it was not yet quite dusk, I saw him turn on the light.

A CLOSED DOOR
— Geoff Woodbridge

HE stood in front of the huge black Edwardian door awaiting an answer. The frosty morning air crept closer into his bones sending a shiver down his spine. He'd regretted that Christmas hair cut the minute the clippers touched his neck. His head now felt numb with cold. He pulled this scarf closer to his face as wintry breath made a hazy mist. The door opened. Fran stood there in a long cream coloured woollen housecoat. Her long copper hair clinging to her porcelain face. Her green eyes were red sore from the tears but they smiled independently of her lips. She looked beautiful. James stepped forward, climbed the steps to the doorway and held her tight, pressing his face against her chest, hearing her heart pounding. He loved her, but they had always only been friends, ever since they first met at University in Edinburgh some years earlier; it all seemed like a lifetime ago.

'I can't believe he's gone Jim' she said, closing the door behind him.

'I'm sorry, and I'm sorry I wasn't here for you. It must have been awful.'

'We all tried to help him, but he wasn't interested. He was obsessed and wouldn't listen to sense. I've tried going over things in my head, over and over, but I should have tried harder to make him listen'

'You tried Fran. Nothing could have helped.' James took off his coat, dropping it over the arm of chair in the hallway. The house was an Edwardian Terrace and probably worth a fortune. It was Fran's parents home. They'd threatened to sell up and buy something smaller but with the current state of the market, they left Fran in charge while they spent the frosty months soaking up the winter sun in the Balearics.

'Do you want to watch his diary? His last words?' She asked. James nodded hesitantly.

The room was a mess and a total contrast to the rest of the house, which was immaculate throughout with antique furniture, grand paintings and expensive looking vases, complimentary to its period. There were several empty pizza boxes containing stale crusts and slices of what looked like it was once tomato. DVD disks, magazines, unwashed clothes and beer cans were scattered across the floor creating a carpet of trash. The room had a musty thick odour, sweet and pungent. His bed was unmade with sheets turning a dull shade of grey from their original Egyptian White. Clothes fell out of the wardrobe like a single entity clinging to the floor, pulling itself to safety. Whether this was a statement of his disinterest and rebellion against his parents, a cry for help or just plain and simple laziness, it was a mess and it smelt bad. Amongst the chaos, in the centre of the room sat a gleaming silver laptop, its logo pulsing with light as it promoted its own existence.

James approached the laptop, lifting the lid. A chime sang out as it sprung to life.

'It's on the desktop. I can't watch it again. I'll get us some coffee.' Fran said, backing out of the room, closing the door.

There were a few icons on the desktop of the laptop. Various software applications, 'Things to do', 'documents', a media file called 'il campo' and another by the name 'last words'. James highlighted the file and hit the double click. Toby's face appeared. He looked older, tired, unwashed and frankly, a mess. James remembered Fran's younger brother as always being full of life. A strong, athletic, confident chap; honest and trustworthy. Flame red hair and a square jaw. A great person to meet, and could always be seen as he held court, the centre of attention at any party, but here, on the laptop he looked like he'd had the life and soul sucked out of him; his eyes were black and tired, his hair lank and dirty. His skin looked washed out and grey. James watched the screen.

This is my last entry. I wanted to make a document, a recording of what had happened as a word of warning and to explain to my friends and family as to why I acted in such a manner. It's difficult for me to express my feelings right now as my mind is only in one place and it's very difficult to get out of my head.

I'll start at the beginning, where all good stories begin. It was Stuart who introduced me to her. I'd been visiting my old friend, Stuart. I the past, he'd always been stable, safe and solid in his relationship. He'd had some problems at home, recently split with his girlfriend and on top of this, lost his office job. We'd had a few drinks and had been chatting for some time. 'Toby, I need to show you something' he'd said. I smiled, but he was serious. In fact, I'd never seen this expression before, it was a look of guilt and terror and frankly, it scared me. We went into his study, a large room lit by a small lamp and the light from his computer. He showed me a video, he told me he couldn't stop thinking about it, couldn't get the image out of his head. It was obsession. I took the chair and sat the desk and watched as the film began to play.

It was a park. A beautiful sunny day with beams of light flashing though the branches and openings of leafy trees. There was a young child, in a white Victorian dress holding balloons in one hand, and the other held the hand of an old man dressed in a black suit with a huge moustache. There was a child riding a red chopper bike, wearing a Six Million Dollar Man T-shirt, Two girls threw a Frisbee to one another, hot-pants and permed hair. A band played brass instruments dressed in military attire. It was colourful and beautiful, almost blinding and I could feel warmth from the sun. Then the film showed a woman on a bench. She sat watching the world, with a smile of love and contentment. She was beautiful. Dark hair, like chocolate shaving curls, hanging around her shoulders, her olive skin soaking up the sun's rays. Full lips, round cheeks and large dark eyes making her beautiful face as perfect as could be. The film focused on this woman, getting closer and closer. She seemed oblivious to whoever had the camera, instead, watching people go by, enjoying the weather, with joy and happiness. People on roller-boots, a dog wagging its tail, a child on a penny-farthing, a girl jogging listening to a walkman and in the sky, an air balloon passed by with a man in a wicker basket raising a glass of champagne as a toast. They were there for her and she watched and soaked them all in. The camera got closer and closer until all that could be seen was her eye.

I couldn't take my eyes from the screen; it was a collection of magical images, people from a different time and place, brought together for this one moment. Realising my mouth was open, eyes as wide as they had ever been, I looked over at Stuart. His head was in his hands, crying with despair. The screen pulled me away from my friend and once more, I was with her, watching her face, feeling her sunny emotion. Then it ended. The screen went blank and it was over. I gasped and immediately went to hit the play button again. Stuart grabbed my wrist. 'I'm sorry. I needed to know if this would have the same effect on you as it's had on me. I can't think straight. She's all I can think about, but she's a closed door Toby, she'll never let you in.'

I held him in my arms as he sobbed; my T-shirt wet with tears. I put the outpouring of emotion down to the Gin and cleaned my friend up, tissues and a coffee before bidding farewell. Although, not before sneakily copying the media file to my Smart Phone. That was the worst thing I could have done. On the bus home, I watched the file again on the small 3" screen, ear-piece firmly in place, I could hear birds chirping like I was there in the park. I could hear the chain of the bicycle and a swoosh as the child rode past. I could hear the laughter and joyful cries as people played; the sound of happiness and love. But the file had changed, evolved with characters moving differently. The girls in hot-pants were now on the far side of the park, replaced by a young boy on grey shorts and sturdy boots, hands in the air, gazing up at the blue sky, trying to catch the sun. The woman still watched from the bench. She was gazing at me from the screen. I could hear her breathe. Her chest rising as she took each breath, Her heart beating, pounding in my ears. Then I was aligned and my heart beat to the same tempo and rhythm and we became one and I could feel warmth on my own skin as it shone down onto her own.

I was jolted to a halt, as a hand grabbed my shoulder. Two police officers lifted me from the empty bus. The driver, a Polish man pointed and shouted things from behind them. They explained it was the end of the route and wanted to know why I refused to leave the bus. I was confused. They searched my pockets for drugs and after no result, sent me on my way with a shove.

I watched the file later that night, the following morning and every opportunity from that moment on. My girlfriend had left numerous voice messages for me after I'd forgotten to turn up for our anniversary meal. They changed from concern and distress to upset, anger and abuse. Each time I listened but the words passed by and my thoughts were in the park and with her. I spent several weeks walking through the parks in the city, looking for a bench or a sign to find the exact place and location of the film. Would she still be there? I dreamed of finding the park and walking amongst the roller-skaters, the dog walkers, the child with balloons and the woman on the bench. I would take a seat and we would talk, I would charm her and she would love me and we would spend every day together, enjoying life, happiness and the park. Then I would wake up to the reality. I'd lost my job, as I'd neglected to turn up for weeks. My money was running out. I'd become hungry and lonely and the file didn't seem to glow like it did before. It was strange. The park seemed less busy, fewer people playing ball, stray dogs running across the grass, desecrating and barking at the child with deflated balloons. It seemed cold, the few people left were wrapped up, scarves and woollen hats, bitter cold winds, frost even. She was still on the bench, her smile, her eyes and beauty still pulled me in and kept me captivated and alive.

It's only now that I can see that I cannot go on like this. I cannot live like this as it's destroying my life. I can't go on with people ringing and pestering me on the phone, Fran knocking on my door all of the time and the hunger in my belly is unbearable. My skin itches and I have this pain in my head. I just need to be with her, I would be safe and free from the world and this pain.

James watched the screen in horror as Toby raised a knife to his throat and opened up a river of blood, which sprayed out with force, a torrent of life pouring from his neck, pumping and flowing as Toby smiled into the camera, drifting away to another world. It was the last thing that James was expecting to see.

'Jesus Christ' James whispered. The file ended. James hit the x in the corner of the screen wishing he could close the image in his own head just as easily and slammed the lid shut. He could feel his own heart beating fast now. Pulling his sweater over his head, his t-shirt underneath was soaked through with sweat from panic and terror. He took a few deep breaths still staring around the room, the mess he was sitting in and noticed the blood stains on the floor deep in the wood grain. He touched his finger-tips across the floor board. There were some light splatters across the silver laptop. He lifted the lid, noticing specks of blood on the screen and keyboard. Then, he looked at the other icons on the desktop. 'il campo.' He could hear himself say as he moved the cursor and double clicked the file and began to watch the view of a park.

THE WHITE FLOWER
— Jeff Baker

IT was in a pleasant greenhouse in the bright light of day that I first encountered what I now think of as the Keller Greenhouse Horror.

I had received several letters from Professor A___, who showed a familiarity with my work, in particular Wordley Field case, where the thing was in the open air, held in check by the property boundaries. But this promised to be different. For a start there was tangible item as the focus of the nightmare I was to confront and hopefully defeat. The urgent telegram came in the middle of the summer. It read: Hurry. Thing may open by week-end.

I arrived in the small college town surrounded by Kansas farmland a few days later, a gentle breeze doing its best to counter the summer heat. Prof. A__ greeted me warmly at the train station.

"Thank God you have come," he said gripping my hand. "It has not opened yet but it may by to-night."

"Yes," I said. "Your letter outlined your fears. Some sort of flowering plant?"

"A thing from Hell," said Prof. A___ in disgust. "No, not from Hell, but from the jungles where I fear it was the focus of the most abominable pagan rites." He took a breath. "I must get a hold of myself. I must concern myself only with facts." He closed his eyes a moment and shook his head. Then he began again.

"That thing has been the prize of the Department's collection. The newspaper people from the city were out here the last time. I am amazed no one realized the pervasive terror embodied by that obscenity." He stared at me. "Every time that flower opens, someone dies. I believe it has killed three people."

"Three!" I exclaimed.

"Yes," he said. "And there will be a fourth unless you can find some way to thwart it."

In his car on the short drive to the campus he outlined the situation.

"It was a gift to the school around 1906. Initially it was believed to be a variant of the Amorphophallus titanum, the so-called "Corpse Flower.""

I nodded. I had seen one of the Amorphophallus titanum in the conservatory in Brooklyn a few years earlier. They were few and far between.

"Dr. G_____ was in charge of the department then. He was excited that this plant had not actually been cataloged before."

I had heard of him, his works on botany were known worldwide.

"The flower opens only at night. At dusk. Only once in about eight years," explained Prof. A___. "I was an undergraduate at the time. Something about it seemed, seemed wrong." He shook his head again. "We took photographs as it bloomed and took measurements. We didn't have a clue how it pollinated, so we decided to leave it alone. We left the greenhouse. The next morning we found one of the janitorial staff dead on the floor near the flower which had, by that time, closed." He sighed again. "That was in 1911. The janitor's death was assumed to be a heart attack. It was sad, but it was soon forgotten. The flower opened next time in 1919, remember we were still studying the flower, this time its blooming caught us by surprise. The victim was a young girl that time. One of the students, again found collapsed in the greenhouse near the flower in the morning. The diagnosis

{82}

was, again, a heart attack. A surprise, considering her youth. Upon examination of the flower, Dr. G___ realized that it had opened again. He was the one who made the connection between the deaths. Nobody else did, the janitor had been old, at least in his sixties, and a sudden death was not that mysterious"

I smiled slightly; I was nearly that age myself. Prof. A___ continued.

"We realized that there had been an eight-year interval between the two openings of the plant. We were expecting one in 1927. With that knowledge, we studied the plant closely and observed some subtle changes we may have missed the first time. Doctor G___ made plans to wait in the greenhouse, at a safe distance this time armed with a pistol. But to no avail, Dr. G___ became the third victim. Again they said heart attack as the cause."

"Was the plant tested for poison?" I asked.

"Yes," he replied. "We gave that curiosity every test imaginable. It is as different from the titanium as night is from day."

"But," I said, "It may be far more worthy of the ghoulish nickname."

"Yes, it may. Ah! Here we are!" Professor A___ turned his attention to pointing out the prominent features of the campus, a refreshing change from the grim talk of a moment before.

Keller College during the middle of that summer term in 1935 was bright, sunlit and pleasant, even in the Kansas heat. Spread out on the edge of the small town old limestone and new brick buildings in small clusters linked by sidewalks lined with neatly-trimmed shrubbery, the clock tower of the old administration building routinely fifteen minutes late, and the greenhouse, looking streamlined in the daylight, ablaze at sunset, and silvery in the moonlight. The greenhouse, a long, affair with a domed central roof and four long jutting glass wings extending from the dome like rays of a sun, housed cuttings and hybrids and some of the rarest specimens many of which grew in difference to the Kansas climate thanks to the ministrations of Prof. A___ and his dedicated group of graduate students. Marking the edge of the campus was a small, dingy red brick building which Prof A___ pointed out as the maintenance building.

I would, the Professor explained, be staying in the suite of rooms reserved for guests of the College; the dorm itself was largely unoccupied during the summer term. My first order of business, I insisted, was to see the plant.

The wings of the greenhouse were surprisingly large, lined with a long table on each side holding plants of various sizes as well as supplies and gardening tools. The roof was high, extending at least a full story overhead. I noticed several very tall specimens growing nearly to the ceilings in the other wings. There were windows and skylights which could be opened if needed and a small electric fan built into the wall over the wooden door that led to the central room under the domed roof which joined the four wings together. The windows of this wing were shut however, to ensure a tropical climate, and it was here that I saw the white flower.

It was large, nearly two heads taller than I was and thin like a poplar tree after a few years growth. A long stalk grew out of a large pot filled with earth, set there on the fine gravel of the greenhouse floor. Folded tightly over most of the stalk was what appeared at first to be several leaves but on more careful examination were revealed to be the petals of the large flower, extending from about a foot above the plant's base, which would open with the stalk in its center at the appointed time. The most amazing thing about the plant was not its size but its color. It was white, the same pale white I had observed in the mushrooms I had seen growing in yards and forests.

"Do you feel it will open soon?" I asked.

"Within the next day or so," Professor A__ replied.

"And the odor is the same as that of the Amorphophallus titanium?" I asked

"No," the Professor replied. "The Corpse Flower gets its name from the carrion stench it gives off to attract flies and beetles which pollinate it. What pollinates this I cannot say, we have tried unsuccessfully to observe that with no success. But when it opens, the bloom's scent is surprisingly sweet." He smiled for the first time. "I have smelled it myself. But it will not be blooming now. Let us get your bags to your room. You may be staying here a few days."

"And nights," I observed.

The rooms, a small bedroom and a small living room area with a couch and a small cooking area were sparse but not unpleasant, and the screened windows let in a breeze that kept the room cooler than I would have imagined. I sat down at the table and quickly wrote out a letter which I left on the table with the hope that it would be mailed to its addressee if I were not around to mail it. I had made a mental note of the summer hours of the campus library which I intended to make use of if I had the time before my confrontation with the gigantic bloom in the greenhouse.

I had finished a late afternoon meal in the campus dining hall when I encountered Professor A__ again, clutching a sheaf of what looked like newspaper clippings.

"I thought you would want to see these," he said, "I should have given them to you earlier."

The newspaper clippings were from the local paper and the school paper, all articles about the flower as well as the obituaries of the flower's three victims. None of them connected the deaths with the flower. In addition there were a couple of photographs, both of the flower.

"This was taken in 1927," Professor A__ said, indicating one of the photographs. "And this one in 1911. I took it myself."

I stared at the more recent picture. The flower had opened, looking somewhat like a poolside table with an umbrella sticking out of its center. The large, white leaves had unfurled revealing a dark array of fluff which had, upon close examination, dozens, no hundreds of tiny filaments sticking up like tiny feelers. Lights had doubtless been set up and I could see the fan of the greenhouse in the wall behind the flower. The second photograph was darker and less distinct. The flower was open and in the same position. I could not make out any features of the greenhouse except for the edge of one of the tables beside it. The filaments sticking out of the cup were not distinct but the flower stood out a stark, ghostly white against the darkness.

I was able to spend an hour in the library looking up what I could on giant blooms, and was grateful for the Professor's collection of clippings, even if they didn't give me any more information than he already had. At dusk, I met the Professor in the greenhouse and we watched the room grow darker and the flower remain still.

The next day I was able to peruse the library further. I glanced through their books on botany and even an encyclopedia without a reference or photograph of the thing in the greenhouse. I was largely certain I wouldn't find anything but I remembered the Wembley Hotel case where the details and solution to defeating the thing were in a neglected book in the town's small library that no one had looked at for years. Again I studied the obituaries of the three who had died. What had they seen and heard in their last seconds?

At dusk, Professor A__ and I again met at the greenhouse.

"I think to-night the thing will open," he said. "The petals seem to be expanding slightly, but it is hard to tell."

As the sunlight turned to a deep orange and the greenhouse plunged into darkness, Professor A__ turned on a small lamp on one of the tables.

"There," he said. "Do you see?"

I saw. Slowly, steadily the bloom was unfurling. First into a cup shape, then expanding and unfolding into a position that resembled an upside-down mushroom. I could clearly see the inside and the actual flower or flowers, rows of purple and deep green petals pressed together, the tiny filaments rising out about an inch above the mass. The filaments were actually waving slightly although there was no breeze. I moved in closer and that was when I noticed the smell. Sweet. Not like a bouquet, but like some exotic foodstuffs. I brought my face in closer to the flower.

"Be careful!" Professor A__ exclaimed. "Three people have died in that flower's presence already."

I stepped away from the flower and nodded. I took a deep breath of the air in the green house.

"Professor," I said. "It would be best for you to leave and allow me to face this by myself."

"Spend the night here alone?" he gasped.

"You called me here to unravel this mystery solve this problem," I said. "I am quite experienced in the area of delving into the unknown. It would be best if you left me to my own devices."

Reluctantly the Professor nodded, clasped my hand and left the room. I waved confidently as he left the building, hoping that I would be able to tear up unsent, the letter I had written the day previous.

The quiet of the night surrounded me. I could hear and see the small fan whirring in its nook in the wall, but from the outside I could hear no sounds of crickets or the other insects I had noted the night before. I wondered vaguely whether they were being silent out of deference to the flower whose blooming intruded into their domain with its scent and its wrongness. I could smell the sweet odor again and I stepped forward, then back a few feet. In the stillness of the greenhouse the sweet odor was slowly spreading. I looked down at the ground to see if I could observe any ants or beetles brawn by the odor to come and pollinate the thing. But the only thing stirring in the greenhouse was the filaments of the plant and myself. I studied the plant. In the light of the bare bulb it had a lumpy whiteness that was indeed more suited to a mushroom.

I noticed the odor again, queer and sweet as I stood there and stared at the plant, its one huge white bloom facing upward as if in appellation to the stars. I felt slightly giddy and reached out and grabbed the edge of the long wooden table that extended the length of the greenhouse. I had registered immediately that the bloom came just up to the level of the table, but somehow the plant seemed to tower over me and dominate the room. I shook my head and wondered for a moment if this was an effect of the lateness of the hour and my staring at the plant in the stark glare of the light bulb. It seemed to be swelling, blocking off my view of the room and the gravel floor and the door behind it. I realized that I was suddenly staring at the underside of the bloom, its white skin looking more corpse-like than before. I clenched the table and concentrated on its reality, the fact that the table was the same height as the flower.

I felt dizzy, understanding that this was not an effect of the night or my lack of sleep. I shook my head and in an instant I realized that I was now looking down on the scene. I could see the flower from above, a gaping maw of dark purple flowers amid the white and the dark of the room like a tinted photograph. I also saw with a thrill of terror the sight of myself standing before the plant, my left hand extended to the side still firmly clutching the table. I still felt the table in my hand and the firmness of the floor beneath my feet even as I knew that I was also somehow floating, no, extended over the scene.

While I could see myself standing on the ground below I also had a vague visual awareness of the myself that was suspended above the scene, somehow stretched out and connected to the me that was standing there below. Even as my mind flashed over what I had heard about astral projection and the transmigration of souls I suddenly noticed that my vantage point was changing, I was somehow drifting over the massive bloom and also moving slowly downward. All the while the overpowering scent surrounded me like a combination aphrodisiac and anesthetic. I remembered suddenly what Professor A---- had said about not knowing for sure how the monster things pollinate, that he had seen the usual insects and birds flee the bloom when it opened.

I squeezed my hand and looked downward at my solid self—the hand gripping the table top clenched harder. And I felt it! But I also felt my connection with my physical body separating, even as I felt myself being drawn towards the flower. I could no longer smell the overpowering sweet smell from the flower but I still felt the haze of unreality that had earlier overwhelmed me. I realized suddenly that the only thing protecting me was my tenuous connection to my own body and once that was gone, my essence, my soul would be drawn into the flower, possibly to pollinate the unholy thing!

I needed to hang on somehow. Hang on—I could still affect my hand somehow. I willed my hand to grip the table tighter and then I began to drum the table with my fingertips. Slowly at first, but I felt the reality of it from above, even as I only heard the sound as muffled from a great distance. I kept it up. I was able to tap louder and in a rhythm. My descent towards the flower slowed. I saw the flower standing there motionless, an open maw in the night. Then suddenly my eyes watered and with a start I realized that I was on the ground again drumming my fingers on the table the sound had brought me into full wakefulness but the noxious scent surrounded me.

I pulled my jacket over my mouth and nose, held my breath and bolted away from the flower, not turning, certain I would see the horror arise and pursue me through the greenhouse. I nearly tripped but found the small door at the back of the greenhouse and if it had been locked from the inside I would surely have broken it down. As it was, I opened the door raced outside into the warm, dark night and fell on the ground a good distance away from the greenhouse, taking big gulps of air. After a few minutes, I pulled myself to my feet and walked around the greenhouse, as if to patrol it, to keep some unwary innocent from stumbling into that den of death. Through the glass I could see the flower as I left it, still lit by the sole light bulb a gruesome white, like a hellish mushroom. I thought of the manta ray I had once seen. I sat down on the ground facing the greenhouse and waited until dawn.

    I must have dozed, for I woke with the orange sunlight illuminating the greenhouse. Inside I could see the flower had folded, giving it the appearance of a large umbrella waiting to be put back in its stand to await the rain. Three lives, I thought. Three to keep that hideous thing alive. But it would only open this once and it had not pollinated, somehow I knew that.

    I sat and thought to myself. Professor A___ had wanted me to investigate the evil, to stop it somehow. To prevent it from taking any more lives. I thought of the three victims and of how the thing had almost made me its latest kill. My memory filled with the horribly sweet smell from the night in the greenhouse, the smell that had almost been my dirge.

    I walked back to the greenhouse, opening the door and cautiously checking for the smell. When I was certain it was safe I strode to where I had noticed an axe hanging alongside a fire extinguisher. It would take me only a few moments to chop the hideous thing to pieces. I had earlier noticed a pile for burning refuse behind the maintenance building. It would be a simple effort to move the thing's remains to the pile across the yard. A little lighter fluid and the obscenity would never trouble anyone again, except in their nightmares.

BEDTIME STORY
— Thomas Oliveiri

LONG ago the Elvish Queen made war on the trolls. The Queen was tall and cold and beautiful. She pressed many other fey creatures into her service. The mischievous goblins had always worshiped her beauty, her whimsy, and her cruelty, and thus served her eagerly. The centaurs, though drunken and undependable, made fierce warriors in the field, so the Queen enlisted them with promise of wine and slaughter. All denizens of the realm, great or small, were forced to take sides. Last she pressed our folk. Soon black or green clad mercenaries served her, though none survived to receive his pay. Only one group refused— some tribes of pixies, as they could have made little difference, chose to not get entangled in the affairs of their betters. And the Queen did not forget this.

The pixies had their own troubles, and had no dealings with the trolls, their lands, or the Queen's vision of a boundless empire. They stayed to themselves until the war came to them. The pixies long ago had learned, from watching bees build their hives, how to make small beautiful buildings, intricate and strong. Mainly they built with small bits of metal that the trolls coveted for forging weapons. The trolls eventually raided the pixie lands. Although this was dangerous—for many trolls died trying to rob the hives—the pixie's population dwindled and they became as hardened to war as the elves.

They led many trolls into traps tearing the invaders into pieces, using illusions and such strategies as they knew. But many pixies died and the metal the trolls took made increasingly fearsome weapons. So every loss led to more losses.

After long years, a lady of the pixie's court came as an emissary asking the Queen a favor: to let the pixies join the elves, as the elves had offered in the beginning, in exchange for protection.

The Queen, who cherished her grudges, had long since discounted the pixies, and, at first, laughed at the proposal. But then thought better of it, for a whim had taken her (she was as whimsical as she was beautiful).

"I will take your scouts and trap-makers into my legions" she said. "And I will teach you to defend yourselves in a proper way."

The Queen looked at a human mercenary in camp. He came from an impoverished country and his teeth were a loathsome black. And so she continued:

"I will teach you to make your dwellings and your weapons from human teeth. Gold is something you have and that is all that humans want, so you will gives them just compensation. And you, ambassador, will do it yourself—not by proxy."

***

Long ages have passed since then. And the pixies have found many strange uses for human teeth. Their lands are now filled with small fortresses, with such elvish glamors laid upon them that the trolls seldom can break through. Incisors have been made into the blades of the deadliest of weapons and molars the bricks of nigh impregnable fortresses. The pixies pay their tribute to the Queen in pretty, soft, white inlays on the fell, hard, iron swords of her guard.

The pixie ambassador still buys the teeth herself, usually small teeth, which are less likely to be damaged and therefore most usable. And so the number of pixies has dwindled more slowly and they stay safe, in constant vigilance, cloistered within their enameled walls.

THE END.

About the Editor

M. GRANT KELLERMEYER

M. Grant Kellermeyer teaches college writing in Fort Wayne, Indiana where he operates Oldstyle Tales Press – editing, illustrating, annotating, and producing editions and anthologies of classic horror fiction. Always drawn to the macabre, the dark, and the unsettling, he was first entranced by Walt Disney's "The Legend of Sleepy Hollow," after which he consumed as much speculative fiction as he could manage. Michael is mostly attracted to the bald humanity of horror (its will-they-won't-they relationship between romanticism and realism, its philosophy and spirituality, its paradoxical tenderness and vulnerability) rather than the simplistic formula that it is agreeable to mindlessly and sadistically watch another person's trauma unfolding (see: torture porn films, *Saw*, *Hostel*, etc.). Horror to him is both a hateful inevitability and a comforting, vulnerable reality. He typically writes stories that rise from real experiences in his Hoosier upbringing – the uncanny uncertainties of remote Midwestern landscapes – and infuses them with a mixture of peaceful isolation and terrifying loneliness. Michael's most influential horror masters are M. R. James, E. F. Benson, J. Sheridan Le Fanu, Ambrose Bierce, H. P. Lovecraft, Arthur Machen, H. R. Wakefield, Washington Irving, Nathaniel Hawthorne, Mrs Oliphant, and Algernon Blackwood.

Made in the USA
Columbia, SC
31 October 2017